Panom

Zofii i Heleere

na pamiątkę obchodu

Konstytucii 3-ego Maja

Stanisław Skarzyna

7 Mai 2000

ATLANTA
ON MY MIND

ATLANTA
ON MY MIND

by
STANLEY SKORYNA

HOME MUSEUM PRESS
YARDLEY, PA

PUBLICATION DATA
Main entry under title:
ATLANTA ON MY MIND

1. General Science.   2. Biomedical Research
3. Popular works W1 100.3   4. Musical works

I. Skoryna, Stanley C. [Title (DNLM)]

ISBN 0-943100-01-1   96-75498

Advance Research Corp.
Home Museum Press, 1808 Makefield Rd.
Yardley, PA 19067 FAX: (215) 953-1930
In Canada: IND Framework Corp., 27 Heritage Rd.
Maitland, ON K0E 1P0 FAX: (613) 342-7801

Any resemblance of fictitious characters in this book (John Ookk, Brent Ericsson, Jay Greenspoon, David Bates, Scott Mace, Uta Fabian, and Members of the Prutenian Soccer Team) to persons living or dead is purely coincidental.

Printed in Canada for Advance Research Corp., Yardley, PA. Last digit is the print number 98765432

This book is dedicated to
Juan Antonio Samaranch
leader of the Olympic Movement
for the Betterment of Humanity

The Author

PROLOGUE

FIREWORKS lit the sky over Atlanta on this fourth of July, 1996, when a strange-looking plane descended vertically on the slope of Stone Mountain, east of the city. It landed in a secluded clearing in an area known as Wildlife Trails. An extremely tall figure opened the cockpit door and jumped swiftly to the ground. The pilot was dressed in a green skin-tight suit completely covering his body; and his head appeared to be wired to an oversized helmet. After assuring himself that he was not observed, he removed his headgear, revealing a long pale face with regular features and short-cropped dark hair. Without hesitation, he pushed the plane by remote control to the edge of the clearing, and into the surrounding bushes. Obviously relieved, he climbed back into the aircraft and remained motionless, seeming to fall asleep.

The pilot of the plane was a Macrocell, one of the few male clones of humanoid subjects produced on Mars by cell culture; to prevent reproduction the Martians did not want the male clones to remain on Mars. This was the real reason why the pilot, a key person in the underground movement to overthrow the rule of Martians, was dispatched to Earth. The reason given to him by Mara, the leader of the giant Martians was that she had decided that a monument should be erected on Earth, to commemorate her journey, some fifteen years ago. An impossible task for one Man? Not if his supernatural intelligence is taken into consideration.

Atlanta was on Mara's mind as the site for the monument. The choice was obvious: the Centennial Olympic Games were to be held in Atlanta in 1996. No better location could be envisioned to acquaint the millions of Earthians from all over the world with Martian culture. The Martians knew about these events through their interplanetary communication system, more advanced than any known on Earth.

In the nearby Youth Camping Ground, another person found herself unexpectedly in the Stone Mountain Park. This was Uta Fabian, the young coach of the Women's Soccer Team from Prutenia, known historically as Dalmatia, a small country on the Adriatic Sea. Prutenia was separated from the neighbouring Bosnia by the Dynaric Alps. To the South was Montenegro, and to the North the Bosnian territory extended like a tongue, reaching the seacoast and dividing it from Croatia, of which it was a part. So, when Prutenia declared its autonomy in 1995, no one paid attention to the narrow strip of costal land. The life-and-death struggle going on in Bosnia-Herzegovina occupied the minds of all the warring factions. Actually, Croatia was glad

The Stone Mountain

to have a free, internationally recognized port on its southern flank. For Prutenia, the advantage of autonomy was to prevent invasion by Bosnian Serbs, at least for the time being, because it had promised not to get involved in the war.

Uta and her soccer team were sent to the Centennial Olympic Games in Atlanta with the mission of letting the world know that Prutenia existed. This was the idea of the Governing Council, who thought that the people should know that there is a country in the former Yugoslavia where different races and religions live peacefully together. Sending an excellent women's soccer team to Atlanta was the best way to promote Prutenia. The team had won all the competitions because of its new playing tactics, and also due to the leadership of Uta, an enterprising Phys-Ed graduate who was taught by one of the best coaches in the world. So when the team left from Dubrovnik for Italy, where they would board a plane for Atlanta, virtually the whole population came to bid them farewell. Uta was the centre of attention and she was worthy of it. On her arrival in Atlanta, without any previous arrangement, she secured transportation for the team to the Olympic Village. It happened to be the Fourth of July and a day of total confusion. A volunteer, staffing the desk, could not accommodate them in the Olympic Village and, instead, obtained for them a location in the Youth Camping Grounds in the Stone Mountain Park area. Two American soccer players, working as volunteers in the Village, took them by bus, provided by the Atlanta Olympic Committee, to the Stone Mountain Park. It was obviously fate that brought Uta and her team together with the pilot who had landed his Martian plane in the nearby Wildlife Trails.

Coastline of the city of Dubrovnik

CHAPTER 1

WHILE the Martian was resting in his plane in the Wildlife Trails, life in the Prutenian soccer camp was abuzz with activity. Having the skills of different professions and experience in camping, the twelve girls were quick to arrange all the amenities for their stay at the Youth Camping Grounds. They were still under the spell of seeing Atlanta, their first visit to a big American city.

"This is a fantastic place", exclaimed Sumita. "Even if we do not participate in the Olympics, it was worth the trip".

"Don't say that", Uta reprimanded her. "We came here to play for Prutenia and we will do it".

"But we still do not know how to arrange that", interjected Maria, the medical student.

"That's my worry", concluded Uta. "You girls arrange the camp and leave the rest to me"!

Uta spoke with such great confidence that whatever she said was regarded as a "fait accompli". This was the leadership quality which showed through her and her previous accomplishments added to her self-reliance and to the fact that everybody believed her.

"As you saw yesterday" continued Uta, "everything went smoothly. We landed at Hartsfield Airport. Other people might get lost on their first visit to America, but we got excellent service and accommodation in what I was told is the crown jewel of Georgia, a 300-acre park in the middle of some 3,000 acres of natural habitat. And we're not isolated! Just fifteen miles from Atlanta with all the amenities available on site. Can you think of a better place to stay"?

"No", answered a chorus of female voices, with two male voices in the background that belonged to Richard and Michael who came over on the Olympic bus.

"Hi Mike, Hi Richard!" The girls exclaimed.

They were showered with questions: "How did you get on the bus?" "Why didn't you think of bringing your colleagues from the team? There are twelve of us here!"

"I have good news for you", answered Richard. "David, who is in charge of the desk at the Olympic Village Transport Service, told me that you can use the bus until the start of the Olympics. You're lucky! Apparently they have more buses than volunteer bus drivers. Unfortunately, you have no license in Atlanta so we have to drive!"

"We don't mind that" answered Uta, "but I would like to learn how to drive! Bloody Mary was driving an ambulance in Prutenia and this is much trickier."

Richard and Michael

"Bloody Mary", questioned Michael. "Who is Bloody Mary?"

"Oh! This is a joke", answered Sumita. "Mary is a medical student and we call her 'Bloody Mary' because she wants to be a surgeon"!

"That certainly is an esoteric name", said Michael. "I am glad there are no 'Bloody Michaels'".

"There could be, if you were to drink a lot", joked Richard.

"Jokes aside", interjected Uta, "I want to know more about your College Soccer Team. How come you are also Olympic Village Guides? When do you have time to practice?"

At this point, Richard was in a quandary as to how to answer her question.

"Well", he answered hesitantly, being obviously not eager to talk about this subject. "We are alternate members of the College Soccer Team. That means that if one of the players gets injured, we have to be available".

"How can we reach you from the Stone Mountain Park?" Uta continued to question.

"We both have beepers!" he answered ostentatiously.

"Can you get one for us, so that we can call you?" asked Uta jokingly.

"I will certainly try", answered Michael. "We are great friends with David and he has all sorts of gadgets!"

The girls were certainly very impressed, realizing that they had met such well-connected fellows.

"Who is that guy David Bates who yesterday phoned Mr. Brent Ericsson, a manager of the Stone Mountain Park, and arranged the accommodation for us?" asked Jana. "This would be impossible in Prutenia! We would have to go through a hierarchial chain of European-style command. At the end, we probably would spend a sleepless night before a decision is reached!"

"You see", answered Richard, "this is America. If something has to be done, we do not hesitate. David knew that there was absolutely no room in the Olympic Village. Space is so tight that I do not know if we will have room for all the entourage; everybody wants to have Olympic service!

"Oh! We are very happy to be here. There's much more privacy in a 3,000-acre space", Uta quipped. "David told us that some of the Olympic competitions will be held here, including archery, cycling, and tennis. Our girls will meet some of the archers and, like Cupid, pierce their hearts", Uta continued to joke. "How about soccer? Where do you practice?"

"You don't know?!" answered Michael with unjustified self-assurance. "In Athens!"

All the girls were startled. They knew the Centennial Olympics were not being held in Greece. But where is Athens?

Michael was content with their surprised looks. "Athens", he repeated ostentatiously, "the Soccer Capital of the United States."

Uta had never heard of the "Soccer Capital", nor had anyone else.

"Don't worry. Athens is about an hour's drive from Atlanta. The soccer competition will be held in several cities including Washington, but the semi-finals and finals will be played in Athens.

"It must be a classic city", commented Nina, a student of architecture, "especially with a name like that."

"It's not a big city like Atlanta, but it's certainly a beautiful old city, full of antebellum relics", answered Michael. "We have a bus, you must go there sometime."

At this point, it occurred to Uta that if any arrangements were to be made about playing in any competitions, she would have to check out Athens.

"I have your word, Michael", she concluded, "you must be proud to be an American. Everything here moves so efficiently and everybody is so friendly!"

"I am proud", said Michael. "Richard is a Canadian from Montreal."

"You said you're from El Paso in Texas. That is quite a distance from Montreal."

"That is all a coincidence. We went to the same school. Do you know about stochastic chance mechanisms? You are from Prutenia certainly an exotic and distant country, and we are here together in Stone Mountain Park. There is nobody from around here."

"Yes, there is", answered a voice from behind. An elderly man appeared, dressed in a uniform worn by attendants of Stone Mountain Park.

"I am Abercorn Smith", he said, introducing himself. "I am the supervisor of the Youth Camping Grounds; if I can be of any help, let me know!"

The girls were delighted.

"One thing we need is some sort of a stove", replied Uta.

"I will bring you an army camp stove. There is one which was left here by a group of campers and I have it in storage. It's very efficient. Anything else?"

"That is all for now. But before you go, may I introduce you to our friends from the College Soccer Team, Michael and Richard. They can help you to bring the stove."

Abercorn did not look very happy. He was a jovial but proud man, a man who likes to do things himself. "If I need help, I will ask for it", he answered. He left and came back soon after with two men and the stove in a trailer behind his truck. Needless to say he was proud of his achievement.

"If you need anything", he said nonchalantly, "just whistle". You are our Olympic guests. Michael and Richard are local fellows." He sounded slightly jealous of his male-help competition. "Besides, they are from Atlanta and they don't know much about Stone Mountain Park."

"Come to think of it, we need some brickets for the stove", volunteered Lidia, who was in charge of the cooking.

"Well, twelve Amazons should be able to get just about anything by looking at a man. They have some brickets at the Stone Mountain Village store. I am sure they will give you whatever you need. Just smile and tell them you are from Prutenia. They certainly do not know where Prutenia is. That's the way to start a conversation. For me, it doesn't matter where you come from. You are our Olympic guests. I will also try to get you some brickets. Ask these guys to bring you a bus load of brickets. I wonder if they can!" He was ready to leave. While Uta thanked him profusely, other girls began to ask him questions.

"Tell us, Abercorn, what do you have at Stone Mountain Park? You know we are completely new here."

Abercorn was very proud to comment while the whole group, including Richard and Michael, listened.

"There are many things here! It is a microcosm of America. Five items are a must: Stone Mountain, with its historical carving, the Antebellum Plantation, the scenic railway trip around the mountain, the Paddlewheeler Riverboat trip, and the Wildlife Trails. There are many other things too numerous to mention.

"Could you show us all of this?" asked Uta.

"Of course", answered Abercorn, "I would be delighted."

In the meantime, the girls got Richard and Michael to help them around the camp. Uta marked out the camp limits and the tents were installed in the proper locations, including the large tent for dining and meetings. A clothesline was installed between two posts for drying the laundry. Electrical outlets and shower and toilet facilities were pre-arranged at the site. Washing was a problem but Abercorn suggested that he would bring them washbasins which could be connected to a water pipe outlet. At some point, they saw Abercorn's truck with a table in it.

"What is that?" inquired Helena.

"This is an American invention", announced Abercorn. "It is a dining table for people like you. You won't have time to wash dishes. You see, the table has two disposal containers underneath the top, which opens in the middle: one for paper dishes and a second one for plastics. Both containers are equipped with battery-operated grinders, which start when you push a button when closing the top of the table. The plastics and the paper dishes are converted into powder for recycling. Please let me know when the containers are full, so I will exchange them."

Wanda, the food technologist, was amazed. "This will make our camp life much easier! We need a lot of time for soccer practice!"

They all said they would recommend the gadget to their mothers.

Abercorn did not want to leave immediately. He helped them install a post on which the white and green Prutenian flag was hoisted.

"Tell me a little something about your country", he said. Richard and Michael also listened attentively when Uta spoke about Prutenia. Evening was at hand so they made a campfire on a flat rock.

"It is difficult for me to describe the location. It is a beautiful country on the coast of the Adriatic Sea. We have

21

lots of fish of all types. We will invite you sometime to do a little fly-fishing."

Abercorn got excited. "Really?" he asked. "I am a fly-fisherman. The only country outside the U.S. and Canada where I have been is Vietnam, and it wasn't enjoyable there, to put it mildly!"

"You must come to Prutenia", exclaimed Anna, whose father was fisherman. "I will show you fish that you have never seen before."

From that moment on, Abercorn became their best friend and advisor. Tara, who studied music, got her accordion out and, with the flickering fire lighting the surroundings, they sang Croatian folk songs. The evening ended on a romantic note, as the girls thought about their far-away country and some of them could not help crying.

* * *

CHAPTER 2

THE NEXT day, Uta suggested to Jana and Sumita that they take a walk in the area surrounding the Youth Camping Grounds. Although all the team members were friends of Uta and she tried not to make any distinctions, Jana, who was a brilliant goalie, and Sumita, who played centre forward, were closest to her when planning strategy for the game.

"We have to determine exactly where we are located in the Stone Mountain Park." Uta said to her two teammates. "According to Abercorn, we live in an American paradise. I was told that nearby there is a wildlife park. I have always been interested in wild animals and plants. Let's go and explore it."

While the rest of the team was engaged in camp activities, the three girls walked up to Robert Lee Boulevard, passing a large building with the inscription "Coliseum". They had no idea what it contained.

They past it and entered a natural habitat of wildlife and a labyrinth of trails. They were amazed by the variety of plants and trees and were unaware that they were exploring the well-protected reservation of the original fauna and flora of Georgia. They also saw two deer crossing their path. They soon came across a small clearing in the woods and saw something that was least expected: a small aircraft of unusual shape, sitting at the edge of the forest.

"Look at the motors on this plane", exclaimed Jana who was an engineering graduate, "some of them are positioned vertically and other horizontally." She started to analyze the construction of the strange plane, its cockpit and short wings.

"If it had blades, I would think it was a helicopter" continued Jana. "Obviously, it has vertical take-off and landing capability; there is no landing strip here. It must be some sort of VTOL!" concluded Jana.

"But what is a plane doing here, in the middle of nowhere?" interjected Sumita. "The Americans are always full of ideas and surprises. I bet that the aircraft is positioned to distribute leaflets or some other form of advertising over the city or perhaps to perform aerobatics? Don't forget that we are located on a much higher level than the city of Atlanta, so the position of the plane is correct for whatever it is supposed to do in the sky over Atlanta."

"You know, girls", said Uta, interrupting the conversation, "I must congratulate you on your determination to speak English among yourselves. You remember that when we landed at Hartsfield we promised ourselves not to speak

Croatian in order to improve our vocabulary and skills in English, and you are certainly holding to that promise. As far as the plane is concerned, I have a different idea. It must be from somewhere else; there are certainly better and safer spots to land than the Wildlife Park. I don't think they allow planes to land here, even if the Olympic Committee says so. The person who flew in here obviously did not want to be seen for some strange reason. We do not know his objectives; they may be good or bad. They are unknown to us and since we are complete strangers, we'd better leave. We may be the first people to be questioned and we should not get involved in something dangerous or undesirable."

Uta expressed her usual cautiousness, typical of good leaders; it became evident that she was also ambitious and enterprising. She no sooner finished her sentence, when a very tall man emerged from the woods behind the aircraft. He was dressed in a skin-tight green uniform completely covering his body except for his head. He was standing beside the plane, completely motionless, leaning against a tree, as if waiting for the girls to start a conversation. He definitely appeared friendly and rather scared, more so than they. After a few minutes of silence and mutual inspection, Uta decided to say something; here was a man much taller than her six-feet-four-inches, and this fact appealed to her. "There are so few men taller than me", she thought.

"Hi, stranger! Can we be of any help? You seem to be sort of lost here! We are also foreigners, but if we can be of any help, let us know!"

The man was still silent. He looked around as if to make sure that nobody else was listening and began to speak slowly with an accent that appeared to the girls to be different.

"My name is Ookk. I come from a different planet. Believe it or not, I came here from Mars; not directly, but my spacecraft is from Mars and I flew here from New Mexico with a mission. You tell me that you are also foreigners; I recognized it by the way you talk. Where are you from?"

Uta became the spokesman for the girls. She explained to the stranger as well as she could where Prutenia was and why they had come to Atlanta.

"We also have a mission", she said. Our purpose is to make Prutenia known to the Olympic World; our group is a soccer team which hopes to participate in the Olympics. We want to show that not everybody from the former Yugoslavia hates other people and is ready to fight. In Prutenia, nobody fights except when they play soccer, and this is of course a 'gentlemanly' fight", she added with a smile.

"Our country was recognized by the United Nations only last year. Do you know Butros Ghali, the Secretary-General of the U.N.? He is good but slow to act; it is not his fault because he has to ask practically everybody in the world for permission to act. The whole of the United Nations cannot agree on anything. That is one of the problems in Bosnia!"

Uta was getting passionate in her speech to the stranger, forgetting that she should ask him some questions. "He says he is from Mars", she thought to herself; "How come he speaks such good English, better than mine?"

"Tell me, Ookk, you certainly have a strange name. One thing I must ask you is, where did you learn English?"

"Oh, that is a long story! We have schools on Mars, and they are very specialized. Anybody who wants to learn an Earthian language has several choices. I chose English, or should I say, my mother told me to choose it; the prerequisite is Latin because there are many English words of Latin origin. So I first learned Latin, and then English. As you can see, my English is quite good."

Uta was not convinced that Ookk came from Mars. She did not know where New Mexico was. In any case, here was a man speaking perfect English and, what was even more important to her, he was at least one foot taller than her. She had never met a young man much taller than her. "This seems to be a problem for all tall girls, including models", she thought. Sometimes they would date shorter men but, generally, they preferred someone at least of equal height. These thoughts convinced Uta that she had found someone who could be her escort during her stay in Atlanta.

Jana and Sumita were listening attentively to Uta's conversation with Ookk. They were even more doubtful about Ookk's story; however, since Uta did not press any further questions, they remained passive. This was their second day in America. In Central Europe, even to some extent in Western Europe, the average person believes that anything is possible in America. Reading the glossy magazines and listening to TV and radio, they are quick to accept almost anything. They saw the "Dynasty" series as a typical story of a well-to-do American family. They didn't realize that the lifestyles depicted in the show were far from average and that it is the dream of all Americans to live in higher income brackets. It was not surprising that the girls, being rather gullible, did not enquire further into the background of the stranger. However, they also read about kidnappings, rapes and other horrors which can happen to travellers all over the world.

Nevertheless, curiosity prevailed. Jana did not want to be outdone by Uta and she invited Ookk to come the next day to their camp.

"I would not know where to go", answered Ookk. "This is my first day here. I do not know exactly where I am. How do you expect me to come over to your 'camp'?"

"I will gladly come over and bring you to our camp", Jana suggested.

After this invitation was issued, Ookk became pensive. He was trying to recapitulate in his mind his first meeting with Earthians. He sort of liked the girls' appearance and their friendliness. "They claim they are also foreigners here." He thought "Perhaps I should join them; it may be better to be in the company of strangers, rather than with local people; there is less likelihood of questions being asked if you are not alone. The tall girl (did she say Uta was her name?) said that they also have a mission in Atlanta. Their mission is different from mine but maybe we can combine our efforts. Uta seems to like me and she, obviously, is the leader of the group."

"Well", he said, "why don't I go with you now. How far is your camp? I also have to secure my plane, but that can be done later."

The girls were delighted with his response. "Why don't we walk you over", responded Uta. "Do you have any other clothing besides what you are wearing? You look rather unusual!"

"This is my spacesuit", replied Ookk, "it protects me against cosmic radiation. We do not need it on Mars and I suppose I do not need it on Earth. However, I have no other clothing."

Ookk's arrival at the camp in his strange attire was dramatic, to put it mildly. The girls asked Uta hundreds of questions.

"Who is that man? Why did you bring him here? Is he going to live here?"

Uta was laconic in her answers but she counted on the goodwill of her companions, who were always willing to help strangers.

"Listen, girls", she intoned. "This man's name is Ookk. He is a stranger here like ourselves and he needs our help. We have a spare tent and we can put it up for him. He is a pilot and he will bring his plane over here. But first we have to provide him with some food and clothing."

The girls immediately put her plan into action. They put up Ookk's tent, equipped with a hammock, at the other end of the camp. Ookk then laid down in his tent and fell asleep without eating anything.

Towards the evening, Uta peeked into his tent and noticed that he was sitting on the grass.

"Hi, Ookk! May I come in? I would like to talk to you."

"As you probably noticed, I am in charge of this camp. I have to explain to the girls who you are and what you want to do. They will accept whatever I say, if they know it is for a good cause. Are you really a Martian?"

"Not exactly, but I am from Mars. I am a male Macrocell. I will explain to you what that means!"

"OK! But you said you came here from New Mexico. Excuse my ignorance, but where is New Mexico?"

"Well, as the name indicates, near Mexico. But to answer your question, that is, how I came here, is a long story. There are two races of people living on Mars. The original Martians, compared to me, are giants. There are only a few hundred of them still living, all females. The second race living on Mars are Macrocells like me, who were developed from cell cultures. There are hundreds of thousands of us and the Martians use us for labour in different factories, like food production, tissue cultures, and communications."

"Almost all Macrocells are females because the Martians do not want us to reproduce, so they did not want any cell cultures that would produce male Macrocells. They are afraid that, eventually, we would rule Mars. We secretly developed a method to produce male Macrocells and I am one of them. The Martians do not know about this, but they suspect that something is going on."

"I am the leader of an underground movement, which was formed to overthrow the Martians. So, you understand that if I stayed on Mars, I could have been condemned to death as soon as the Martians identified me as a male Macrocell. That is why my mother, Mara, who visited Earth

30

before, invented a reason to send me there. When I was being prepared for my cosmic journey, I was told that my task is to build a monument on Earth to my mother, although the real reason is that they did not want me to stay on Mars. However, I figured that this was an excellent chance for me to get away from something that, in reality, is a labour camp. Apart from any danger in staying on Mars, I also wanted to see what I could do on my own."

"This really is a long story, Ookk", interjected Uta, "but please continue so I will know exactly your origin."

"After the big cataclysm, when the surface of Mars was burned out by solar radiation, all the Martians living on the surface vanished. Only those who were living inside Mars survived. They started tissue culture, hoping to produce new Martians like themselves, but the experiment failed. The tissue culture produced only miniature beings, by comparison, which are Macrocells like myself. However, our intelligence is very high and we all believe that eventually we will take over and rule on Mars."

"This is fascinating", said Uta, "but what are you going to do on Earth, a totally different and, to you, unknown environment."

"I have an inherent ability to do many things on my own. Mara wants me to build a monument to acquaint people with life on Mars. I have to think what structure I can build. Maybe you and your friends can help me develop an idea acceptable to Earthians!"

"Well, I told you", answered Uta, "that we are also strangers here. In a sense, we too have to do something unusual to complete our mission. Tell me, Ookk, how strongly do you feel that you have to build a monument to your mother? Is it that you want yourself to do it, or do you have to because you were ordered to do so?"

"It is both. We, as Macrocells, have been indoctrinated since childhood to follow orders. This brainwashing still influences me. So, in effect, I believe I have to do what I was told. On the other hand, I would also like to do on my own something useful. If this monument serves a good purpose, I would have the feeling that I had accomplished something without being ordered to and that would give me great satisfaction!"

"Uta, perhaps we can work together", continued Ookk. "Your task is to show the world the value of peace. My task could be to show Earthians how they can better themselves. Perhaps the monument my mother asked me to build can somehow reflect this theme."

What he was saying appealed to Uta; it was logical and straightforward. He understood that having been ordered all his life, he had to assert himself. At the same time, he always remembered the orders of the giant Martians and this remained in his consciousness as a remnant memory.

Uta was happy that they had had this conversation and felt more sympathetic towards Ookk's objectives, in spite of the short time that she had known him.

"Tell me one more thing, Ookk" said Uta, "how old are you?"

"Well! The Martian day, which we call 'sol', is 30 minutes longer than the Earthian day; that adds 178 hours or, roughly, 15.5 days per year. On Mars, I was thirty years old, so here I would be thirty-one!"

Uta was amazed with his knowledge and his calculations. It obviously mattered to her how old Ookk was if he was to become her companion. "Let's plan now what we will tell the group."

"Whatever you want", replied Ookk. "You now know the whole story."

When they emerged from Ookk's tent, Uta called a meeting of all the campers to explain Ookk's presence.

"Listen, girls, as you know, I invited Ookk to stay in our camp", she stated. "He will be our guardian. He can also be our pilot; he has a very good plane which he will bring to the camp and that will help us with transportation if there are emergencies. Let's have supper and then we can get his aircraft over here."

The girls were amazed by the speed of her actions. They were all excited about the news and the presence of a new person in their camp. They were sizing up Ookk carefully in his unusual uniform. "What is it for? Is it some sort of a flying suit?"

Uta was quick to suggest that they get a Prutenian soccer uniform for Ookk, so that he would conform with the rest of the group. As a temporary measure, two of the girls sewed additional material on to a pair of Uta's pants to make them longer. An extra-large white shirt was found; it barely covered Ookk's waist but it worked. Uta suggested to him that he go back into his tent and change his uniform. He did this very quickly and with great satisfaction. When he appeared on the field in his Prutenian outfit, everybody applauded. He was a towering figure and commanded both respect and awe.

Following this, Ookk, along with Uta and Jana, went back to transport his aircraft to the camp. They found it in good repair. Ookk pulled it out of the bushes and asked the girls to get on board and soon they were off on their first Earthian flight to the Youth Camping Grounds. It normally would be a two-minute flight, but on Uta's request, Ookk showed them from the air the entire Stone Mountain Park with all of its surrounding acres of forest.

"It is a marvellous view", exclaimed Jana, "look at all those wonders! There's a paddle boat on the lake, and on the side of the Stone Mountain there are some gigantic carvings."

All this was new to them. "We must explore it all on foot. It would be a pity not to see one of the most exciting parks in the world!" exclaimed Uta.

"I hope I can go with you, now that I have your team's uniform", quipped Ookk.

"Oh", said Jana, "we will gladly include you in our activities. It would be a good excuse for us to see everything, because we have to show it to you."

"Well", answered Ookk, somewhat scared, "I can keep my identity secret, at least for now. Eventually, everything will become known. However, let's wait for an appropriate time, otherwise people will think you are joking."

**Carving of confederate heroes on
north side of Stone Mountain**

"I thought of that", answered Jana, "but you are so tall that you become immediately noticeable and people will start to ask 'Who is that man'?"

"You have to invent a story. You can say that you brought with you the tallest man in Prutenia", he laughed.

When they finally landed at the Youth Camping Grounds, bedlam broke out among the girls. Fortunately, there were not many strangers around, but some people came to look at the unusual plane.

"I think that you should explain to them how your unusual plane works", said Uta.

"I will try to make it as simple as possible. The advantage of this plane is that it can go from point to point because it's a VTOL and does not need to go to an airport or refueling. It has Vertical Take-Off and Landing systems and uses a compound similar to ordinary gasoline. This plane is really a sky car because one can choose the time and place of departure as well as destination for a non-stop flight. The aircraft is equipped with eight engines, two of them mounted on each of the four nacelles. Synchronized counter-rotating fans provide the power for vertical takeoff and hover. Once the desired altitude ceiling is reached, a system of duct vanes transmitting the thrust from these fans is redirected by computer for horizontal flight. A great advantage of the plane is that it is equipped with a muffler system, which reduces the noise to the acceptable level of a truck engine. It can fly at 400 miles per hour with a range of 700 miles. The ceiling is 40,000 feet. This is a complex system which the engineers made simple and efficient."

"Ookk", Jana interrupted, "tell us what this type of plane could be used for on Earth?"

"I do not know enough about your transportation system to answer this question", said Ookk, "but when you have to fly to a destination without going to the airport, this type of plane comes in handy."

"I can think of one use", proposed Sumita, "Emergency Ambulance Services. In our country, an ambulance has to go through city traffic or over rough country roads and valuable time is lost. It would be easier to fly the patient from his or her home to the hospital."

"But in America, they have air ambulances", questioned Maria.

"Yes", answered Uta. "But an air ambulance has to start from the airport and a lot of time is lost."

"Oh," exclaimed Ookk, "so, maybe on Earth I can become an ambulance driver!"

"Let's not joke", concluded Uta, "it is getting late and we should pull the plane to the edge of the camp. Supper is ready."

In the course of their conversation, which continued after they had eaten, it became apparent to Uta that it would be foolish not to disclose Ookk's identity. His sudden appearance with a strange plane, his attire and behaviour, and the fact that he was asking all sorts of simple questions, indicated even to a "stranger to America" that there was something unusual about this man. Uta decided to tell the whole truth, all the facts that she knew. She told Ookk in

Prototype of skycar similar to Ookk's aircraft with its inventor Dr. Moller

advance about her plan so that he would be prepared; she then took a deep breath and made her speech, which Abercorn was also listening to.

"Girls, you will be happy to hear that we have a very important person among us, namely Ookk. I am pleased to say that we are the first group on Earth to greet a visitor from Mars. It was a long journey for him, from one of Mars' satellites called Phobos to a landing place in New Mexico. He then came with this plane to Stone Mountain Park. He has a specific task to carry out in Atlanta and I hope we can help him. He promised me that he would also help us in all our undertakings during the Olympics."

Following her short speech, complete silence reigned for a few minutes. The Prutenian girls were quite startled by her announcement. They always took Uta seriously, but saying that this man was from Mars sounded quite outlandish. A barrage of questions followed, directed at both Ookk and Uta. Nobody was completely satisfied with her answer. The girls spoke to one another, proposing all sorts of alternative possibilities concerning Ookk and his "task" on Earth. Many people thought that this was some sort of cover-up for the real facts. Uta interrupted further talk by asking them to continue their discussions in private and not to disclose the truth to an outsiders.

"We couldn't do it anyhow", quipped Maria, "nobody would believe us! You wouldn't either, if you were told that you had a 'guest' from Mars!"

The only person who did not doubt the story was Abercorn. Being a believer in technology and space travel, he thought that everything was possible. He was certainly impressed with Ookk's tallness as well as his aircraft.

"You're right", concluded Uta. "All that Ookk is asking is that this information remain confidential among us, so that people won't think we are crazy. I think we should respect his wishes."

With these thoughts, the group dispersed, but discussions could be heard in their tents well into the night.

***

CHAPTER 3

THE next morning, Ookk was the first to wake up. Since everybody else was asleep, he thought it was a great opportunity to explore the surrounding wilderness. The only area of Stone Mountain Park that he knew was the Wildlife Trails. He proceeded through a maze of trails, which were in reality a nature park with animals, such as deer and fox, which regularly crossed his path. None of them seemed to be afraid of him and two deer actually approached him, obviously used to getting food. However, since he did not know what they wanted, he got somewhat scared and ran further into the bush. In the afternoon, a heavy rain came down which stopped any further exploration. He was getting tired and proceeded to build himself a sort of a nest, high on the branches of a huge tree. "This", he thought, "will protect me from any of these creatures." With the rain continuing, he lay down on his Earthian bed and fell asleep.

In the meantime, the daily activities in the Prutenian camp were going on. After breakfast, Michael and Richard arrived with the Olympic bus. They were greeted exuberantly by all the girls.

"Hi, fellows, where are the friends that you were supposed to bring along?"

"They couldn't make it", answered Michael, "but I brought you something interesting from the Olympic Village: funny charts listing energy expanditure in various activities including sports. I also brought you the bus."

"Thank you Mike." answered Sumita. "We need the bus. We will study your charts and practice various activities."

"That's excellent", exclaimed Sumita. "We want to see the Olympic Village and we need transportation."

With all the excitement surrounding the arrival of the bus, no one noticed that Ookk was absent until Uta went to his tent to look for him. Not finding him there, she screamed out in surprise.

"Girls! Ookk is not here!"

"Don't be too concerned", answered Jana, "he will find his way back."

"Who is Ookk?", asked Michael.

There was a moment of hesitancy in her voice when Uta replied:

"You fellows do not know our guest Ookk; he is from Mars and will help us in our tasks."

She sounded so serious that everybody paused in their conversations. Her words created a concern but mostly laughter.

"The poor fellow is somewhere in these woods and nobody is ready to assist him", she continued.

"Let's look for Ookk", sounded the voices.

"Who is Ookk?" Michael repeated his question.

Richard and Michael began talking between themselves in a low voice? "From Mars?", thought Richard, "This girl is crazy." They thought this was a good joke on the part of this strange team leader from Prutenia. They had never before heard about their country. And now, Uta claimed they had a guest from Mars. "Ha! Let's see him!" demanded Richard.

When Jana announced that she had looked for Ookk in the surrounding woods and could not locate him immediately, Richard thought that this confirmed his view. "Good", he said, "show us Ookk and we will believe you."

Uta wanted to direct the conversation towards the search for Ookk. She was never short of answers.

"OK, fellows. We can't show you Ookk right now but we can show you his plane. Let's go see it! Seeing is believing!" With these words, she led the whole group to the place where Ookk's VTOL was hidden. Michael, who was mechanically minded, immediately started to examine the aircraft. He even tried to get inside, but was unsuccessful; the plane was locked.

A lively discussion about Ookk and his plane ensued. The group continued talking about Martians, Martian planes, and everything else they had heard about Mars. For a moment, Uta thought that Ookk might be sleeping inside a

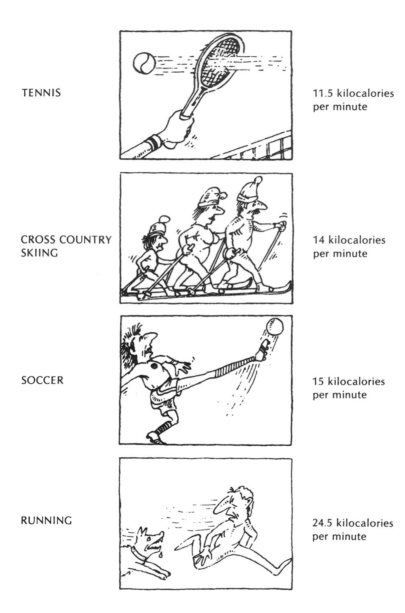

TENNIS — 11.5 kilocalories per minute

CROSS COUNTRY SKIING — 14 kilocalories per minute

SOCCER — 15 kilocalories per minute

RUNNING — 24.5 kilocalories per minute

Energy expenditure in recreational activities

hidden part of the cockpit, since it was locked. She climbed a nearby tree and inspected the remaining portion of the cockpit. "No, there is no Ookk here", she announced.

Richard and Michael got ready to return to the Olympic Village and promised to come back the next day.

"Can you guys stay here all night?" pleaded the girls.

"We have to be back at the Village. We'd better get going. We certainly will come back tomorrow to see him", answered Michael. Ookk is his name, you said? That's a really strange name. I think it's also a good joke. Let's go to Mars together; in good company, Martians will not swallow us. We may be too big for them."

The girls didn't like this sort of joking. They took Ookk's absence too seriously.

"You guys could not stand up against us in the field", shouted Sumita. "Let's have a game tomorrow. Bring your friends and we will see how the play develops!"

Michael took a second look at the girls and started to feel sorry that he ever brought up the subject. It would be embarrassing to lose against a women's team, he thought. So he tried to change the conversation to a more amenable subject.

"You know, there's a fantastic place to dance in town. Have you been "Down the Hatch" in the Underground? It is just past the Five Points. We'll get some of our teammates and we will all go together."

The girls were excited. Everybody forgot about Ookk, except Uta, as they began making plans for the dance.

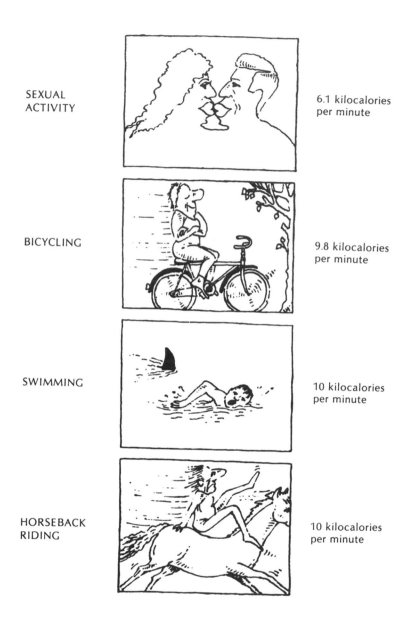

SEXUAL ACTIVITY — 6.1 kilocalories per minute

BICYCLING — 9.8 kilocalories per minute

SWIMMING — 10 kilocalories per minute

HORSEBACK RIDING — 10 kilocalories per minute

Energy expenditure in recreational activities

The day was not conducive to any search in the woods – the rain was still pouring down. Uta held a meeting and she decided that the girls would walk to the Wildlife Trails, on the eastern slope of Stone Mountain Park, and that they would remain 50 yards apart to search for Ookk. Unfortunately, they did not have compasses and there was a possibility that the searchers might get lost. They were instructed to call each other frequently. Unfortunately, they also did not have twelve whistles to communicate with each other. They had not expected to be equipped for a search expedition when they had come here to play soccer. Uta, Jana, Sumita, and Maria were appointed team leaders and they proceeded into the woods. They agreed to meet in the camp in two hours.

Uta soon realized how difficult the task was, particularly because she had to keep a relatively straight line in order not to get lost; she called out frequently to her three team leaders and in turn heard their calls, the echoes were somewhat muffled by the heavy rain. Unfortunately, they had well-fitted raincoats, which were also of great help when trying to get through the bushes.

They returned to the camp two hours later, tired and hungry. Their pretty faces were marred by scratches and disappointment at not finding Ookk.

In the meantime, Abercorn came to the camp to find out what all the commotion was about. Uta explained that Ookk was lost in the woods most likely on the eastern slope of the Mountain. He promised to help them in their search once the police had been notified that a person was missing.

BOWLING

4.9 kilocalories
per minute

GOLF

8.5 kilocalories
per minute

WALKING

8.8 kilocalories
per minute

DANCING

9.9 kilocalories
per minute

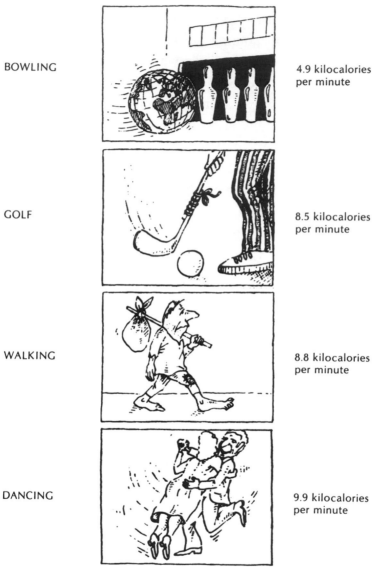

Energy expenditure in recreational activities

To the surprise of the girls, Michael and Richard decided to return and help them to search for Ookk as well.

"Hi, girls", intoned Michael, "have you found your 'Martian' fellow? I really don't believe that you have a Martian hiding in the woods. I have never heard of such a story. It is a good tall tale, but we are too realistic to believe it", continued Michael.

"There is always a first time for everything", said Uta, "Ookk is real. He even told us why he is here. He is the son of Mara, a giant Martian who landed in Canada fifteen years ago."

At that point, Richard's face lit up. "Did you say Mara?"

"Yes. Why?"

"Well, now I believe you. Actually, I saw Mara's landing in Ontario. She was very ill and my father washed her stomach out with water from the creek, using a hose."

"Why would he do that?" inquired Uta.

"Well, she had a bleeding ulcer. Apparently, if you wash out the stomach with cold water or swallow ice, the bleeding stops. This is what they do in the hospitals. At that time, I was only four years old, so I don't know all the details, but my mother told me all about it later."

Now Uta's face lit up!

"What a small world! So, you actually saw Ookk's mother! Now I believe everything that Ookk has told me! It is true!"

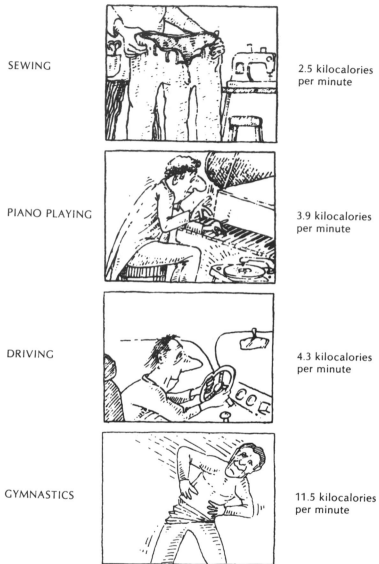

SEWING — 2.5 kilocalories per minute

PIANO PLAYING — 3.9 kilocalories per minute

DRIVING — 4.3 kilocalories per minute

GYMNASTICS — 11.5 kilocalories per minute

Energy expenditure in various activities

"You know, Uta, there was a book published about Mara's landing. I don't think you can get it. It was fifteen years ago and it probably is out of print. I only remember a song from the book. It is called 'The Departure of Mara'. It was very sad."

"Let's hope that the disappearance of Ookk does not become a sad story", interjected Uta. "It is still raining. Let's have lunch in the tent and decide what to do next."

Most of the girls thought that the police should be called to help them in the search. Jana agreed. She walked with Richard to the telephone and dialled 911.

"We have a person lost in the woods on the mountain", she said. "He is from Mars and we are afraid that something has happened to him, because everything on Earth is new to him. He has not returned since last night."

The voice on the other end of the line became curious. He also noticed Uta's accent.

"You said he is from Mars. Where are you from?" came the question from the other end of the line.

"From Prutenia. I am a member of an Olympic Soccer Team."

"Did you say Prutenia? I never heard of such a country. I have in front of me a list of all participating countries and Prutenia is not among them."

"I know that, because the country became autonomous only last year. But this is beside the point. I am not looking for help for myself. There is a person from another planet who is lost. I am only reporting it; if something happens to him, you will be responsible."

The guy on the phone became angry. "You know, madam, we get a lot of crank calls on this line. Do you know that you have to pay $100.00 if you give false information to the Emergency Service? You'd better have your head examined and then call us back."

"He hung up", said Uta to Richard.

"I think he was annoyed by your accent. Let me call him."

Richard went to the phone and called the emergency service again. He explained the situation in perfect English, using an authoritative voice. To no avail! Unfortunately, the same person answered and once he heard the words "from Mars", he didn't want anything to do with it.

"I believe everything you say. Our regulations state that any person requiring emergency help will get it. You say he is from Mars? If he says he is from Mars does he look normal? Maybe you should call the psychiatric hospital!" he concluded.

At this point, Richard thought of Mark Twain's story about the man who fell into the water and the police did not help him until he started to scream, after which he was arrested for disturbing public order.

"We have to go back to the camp and continue to search for Ookk ourselves", said Jana.

"Do you know where the name Mark Twain comes from?" he asked Jana.

"No!"

"You see, the phrase 'Mark Twain' is a measure of sounding in fathoms on the Mississippi River. Mark Twain's real name was Samuel Langhorne Clemens. He used this pen name – this pseudonym – to commemorate his time spent on the River. It also sounds better for publication", continued Richard.

"Why are you telling me this?" answered Jana. "Actually, if you want to know, two people wrote Mark Twain stories, Samuel Clemens and Isaiah Sellers. They both used the same pseudonym."

"I said this only because I was thinking that Mark Twain was right that to the police or any authorities, you have to give reasons or vocabulary that they understand. They do not necessarily understand unless everything is 'according to regulations'" complained Richard.

By the time they arrived back at the camp, Uta had a plan ready for Ookk's rescue. But Abercorn interjected with his own suggestion.

"I don't know what you have arranged, but I believe that it would be better just to find him ourselves and not involve the police. He must be sitting somewhere nearby, scared to death."

"If he were nearby, he would hear us", said Tania.

"In any case, the police might start shooting."

"I am not from here", said Michael. "In Texas and New Mexico, they have coyotes and rabbits. Here they might have bears."

TYPING

3.1 kilocalories
per minute

CARPENTRY

8.5 kilocalories
per minute

SNOW
SHOVELLING

14.7 kilocalories
per minute

DIGGING

15.0 kilocalories
per minute

Energy expenditure in various activities

Uta suddenly became afraid that Ookk might have been attacked by a wild animal. She asked Abercorn for his help.

"I'll tell you my plan. We should fan out in one direction. There are fourteen of us; if we walk twenty-five feet apart, that would cover quite a distance. Then we could comb the adjoining strip, until we find him. Let's select the direction where he is most likely to be. If his plane landed to the east, this is the most likely direction."

Uta put his plan immediately into action. This time, they were smarter; instead of calling "Here" or "Hello", they called his name to one another.

Fortunately, it stopped raining. They decided to wear their raincoats anyway; this made walking a bit awkward, but served as a good protection against thorns and branches. Soon, the woods sounded with calls for "Ookk" and the echo repeated the name many times. The first three trips were unsuccessful. The slope increased considerably on the east side of mountain and it was difficult to climb back. Only on the second trip did Uta realize that they should walk back on the adjoining strip, in this way they would cover a larger area.

On the fourth trip, the girl on the left wing reported seeing the bed that Ookk built for himself. They did not know what it was. An Indian wigwam? But the nest was empty. The girls had good experience from their girl guide days; they soon discovered that the occupant had left not too long ago. There were freshly broken branches and crushed leaves around the nest.

Uta, of course, was the next one on the scene.

"This must be Ookk's house", she exclaimed. She proceeded to move downhill, leaving the rest behind. Soon, she discovered an unconscious figure lying on the ground. It was Ookk. He was motionless and obviously unconscious.

Uta looked tenderly at him.

"Ookk, my dear Ookk." she exclaimed. "I hope you are not hurt!" There was no answer.

The girls and the two boys gathered around Ookk. Michael suggested that they make a "portage" out of the branches and carry Ookk back to the camp. Richard and Michael actually went ahead, making a sort of path by cutting off some of the branches and overhanging vines. Fortunately, Richard had his Swiss army knife with him, with which he could cut even thick wood.

Soon, the stretcher was ready. Ookk remained motionless during the arduous trip. It was bumpy, to say the least, but Ookk arrived at the camp unharmed.

The girls started to apply compresses to his forehead and covered his body with a blanket. That was unnecessary since it was a hot July day. But one could understand their anxiety. Particularly Uta's who openly expressed her feelings towards Ookk.

Michael once again decided to examine Ookk's aircraft since he now believed that it did in fact come from Mars. "It is ingenious", he commented. "Since you said that he came from Mars, he would need some sort of protection in space travel, and this is why he wore that suit. It seems to be much simpler than our astronauts' clothing."

"They are more advanced than we are in everything.", said Uta promptly. "Obviously, they provide for everything; I noticed that there were air openings in front and at the back of the suit for passing urine and feces."

"They must be built just like us", she continued.

Another thing that Uta noticed was a lump on the back of Ookk's head. "Oh!", she exclaimed, "this is why he is unconscious. He banged his head when he fell." There was no bleeding, so no special care was required. But Uta provided it anyhow. She applied ice to Ookk's head with great tenderness and with obvious emotional involvement.

Ookk was transferred from his stretcher to the hammock in his tent. Uta and Michael were sitting at his side when, after two hours, he opened his eyes. He looked at Michael and said: "Who are you?"

He did not appear to be upset upon seeing a stranger, but when Uta approached him to congratulate him in regaining consciousness, his face lit up.

"Uta", he said, "where am I?"

"You are back home, in the camp. This is your new home. You said that you cannot go back to Mars, so you might as well join our Prutenian team and come with use, after the games, to Prutenia." Ookk was too dizzy to comment on this suggestion. For the next two hours, he lay quietly in his hammock.

After resting, he started to tell how he had gotten lost in the woods and how he had built himself a nest and later a shack where he had slept at night. He also related how a dark creature – unfortunately he could not name it – had started to climb into his hut. He got scared, jumped out and began to run until he became completely exhausted. All he remembered was that he had fallen.

"You see, girls", Abercorn concluded, "it takes a Vietnam veteran to find a man in the bush; now I can say that I even traced a man from another planet." Abercorn, as well as Michael and Richard, was now convinced that Ookk was indeed a Martian.

Everybody was happy that Ookk was back, seemingly without serious injury. He was now considered to be a member of the Prutenian family, someone who the Earthian World had thought of as ethereal. No wonder Abercorn was congratulated on his search plan, and his ego inflated to a much higher level.

***

CHAPTER 4

IT TOOK a few days for Ookk to recover from his head injury following his fall in the woods of Stone Mountain. He enjoyed staying at the Prutenian Camp, observing the girls going about their daily routine: preparing meals, washing and exercising. They met some Americans at the neighbouring archery field and convinced them to permit the soccer practice to take place there, when the field was not being used. Naturally, this had to be early in the morning, so the whole camp got up early and off they went for an hour or two of soccer practice. The management of the camp was very cooperative and they even allowed them to build a goal on one side of the field. It was very primitive, made of three long logs, but the size was consistent with the rule, so the net could be spanned across for practice. Some of the archers participated in the team's practice. They were amazed at the girls' skills and agility, and were particularly impressed with Jana who was an exceptional goal tender. Naturally, friendships developed between some of the Prutenian girls and the American archers.

During the past few days, Ookk had plenty of time to think about himself, his past and his future on Earth. Uta had to go to practice with the team, so he was often left all by himself, admiring the beauty of the park, walking around the compound, or lying on the grass and staring at space, where somewhere on the horizon was a star, the place of his birth.

Ookk was determined by now not to return to Mars. When he thought of the long laborious days at the cell-culture factory and evenings spent in secrecy with friends, planning how to overthrow the Martians, his determination to stay on Earth became stronger. Although he was a well-built and desirable man, he had always tried to avoid female Macrocells because he was afraid of rejection or punishment. The women were not allowed to talk to anybody during work; the circumstances not dissimilar to the totalitarian society described by George Orwell's novel 1984. They were also scared to approach Ookk or the few male Macrocells, since the punishment was always severe: death by being brought to the surface of Mars and embalmed by freezing.

All these thoughts went through Ookk's mind as a distant reminder of his past. What was fresh in his mind were the preparations for his departure, when he had been selected by Mara for the journey to Earth. Travel to Earth was in fact not that infrequent. The rockets were built on Phobos, one of the two Mars satellites, the factory being located in the deep dark cave and occupied by thousands of Macrocells. In effect, anybody who was convicted to die was given the choice to work on Phobos instead, with no prospect of returning to Mars; nevertheless, some Macro-cells chose this alternative. It is interesting that on Mars, like on Earth, when people are faced with the prospect of certain death, they choose to live under conditions which are probably worse than death, but which give them a hope for survival.

Ookk recalled vividly the time when he was called to see his mother, Mara, not knowing why she had sent for him. She had been lying on a huge mat, surrounded by hundreds of fearful Macrocell guards performing various duties: bringing baskets of synthetic food, combing her hair, and cutting her nails. Some of them had been simply sitting, waiting for orders transmitted through the Chief Warden.

Mara's orders had been curt: "Go to Earth and build a monument in my memory. I have selected a place, the City of Atlanta where the Olympic Games will be played three years from now. That gives you enough time to travel. I leave to your ingenuity how you will perform this task. I know you can do it. I was very generous to you because you are one of the few Macrocells who can complete this task. I know more than you think about your activities and those of your colleagues but I cannot change history. My oracle tells me that I cannot. So you can go now and complete your mission." Mara's words were still ringing in his ears.

The journey to Earth was actually not as monotonous as he expected because he kept himself busy. Ookk had loads of computerized books that he listened to: geographical information about the Earth's continents and countries, and histories of Western and Eastern civilizations. Later, he concentrated on America, the country where he was going to land. He learned a lot about Atlanta, the Civil War, and current developments. And when he wanted a diversion, he listened to tapes on the Solar System and on the history of Mars as known to Earthians. Actually, this "listening library" was recorded on Earth by one of the "flying saucers" using very elaborate equipment, much more advanced than the current multimedia devices being developed on Earth.

"So, here I am", Ookk said to himself, "in a soccer camp of a Prutenian group which is also new to this country. So far, I have been lucky because I have not been discovered by the Earthian media. What's going to happen when my origin becomes known? Will they believe my story or look upon me as a mentally-ill person?"

So far, everything was going better than he had expected. The landing in New Mexico had gone smoothly. His plane had been unloaded, with the help of Macrocells who manned the space vehicle. He had been supplied with a small quantity of synthetic food and had then said "goodbye" to the Macrocells who departed back to Mars. He had then boarded his plane for the atmospheric flight to Atlanta; only a 100-foot burned-out circle was left on the site for people to wonder about.

The events at Stone Mountain Park had also gone smoothly. He actually had not known where to land near Atlanta, but had selected a wooded area near the city; when he had seen the huge stone mountain, he had not known that he had landed on one of the landmarks of the United States.

What occupied his thoughts most of the time was how his future would develop. He knew he was "in good hands", meaning that Uta and her group would do anything in their power to help him. Their sympathy was the understanding of individuals who were themselves strangers in this country. They understood his feelings as a "total stranger". However, they were unaware of his reading experience and his superior intelligence. They did not know that he could automatically connect two unrelated facts or occurrences and establish a relationship between them, if there was any. In reality, he had an extraordinary research mind. Einstein said once that imagination is more important than knowledge. He was not a psychologist but he conceived that a person possessing a logical mind can "imagine" or visualize the connection between facts which are not obvious to others. He confirmed this fact by repeating what Columbus had demonstrated to his own confreres as how he discovered America: he passed an unbroken egg to his companions around the table, none of them had the imagination to realize that the only way the egg would stand up would be to break it slightly at the base.

One of the key problems that occupied Ookk's mind during his recovery period was his future relationship with Uta. He knew that a lot depended on the outcome. He sensed that Uta loved him, since she demonstrated it so obviously during their short relationship; she was guiding him, telling him how to answer questions, as well as answering questions for him. Sort of taking charge of him, as being a unique member of her soccer team. Ookk appreciated all this greatly; he knew that at least for the time being he would be lost without Uta. However, his basic instinct of independence was telling him that he did not want to be permanently taken care of. Perhaps this feeling was related to his relationship with his mother, where he was constantly told what to do, how to do it and when. Ookk could not possibly tell Uta this, and did not want to. But he wondered what would happen when he eventually told her that he did not want to be taken care of, that he would rather take care of her when he was capable of doing so. With all his admiration for Uta's ability, he wondered whether her dominance would eventually destroy his sense of self, his identity as a Martian who had come to Earth. Even if he were to live here, he thought, he could not become an Earthian because he did not feel as one of them. His past experience would always subconsciously affect his actions, regardless of his future experiences on Earth.

The second question that frequently came to his mind was their sex relationship. Ookk was really afraid that Uta would ask him to make love. He had never had any sexual relationships previously. He had frequent "wet dreams" when he thought about women but he was afraid to approach them. He fantasized himself being surrounded by hundreds of female Macrocells and not being permitted to touch any of them.

Being a keen observer, he saw that Richard and Jana were attracted to each other, and that Michael and Sumita talked with sexual innuendos. He saw how the Prutenian girls flirted with the visiting athletes from the archery team. But he simply could not relate these observations to himself. "I wonder", he thought, "whether the most difficult question is always how to relate the psychological experience to yourself." Ookk had read Freud's theory and Jung's interpretations of it. His own conclusion was that even outstanding scientists propose theories that are most likely based on their own psychological experience and that there is a lack of detachment when comparing other people's emotions to one's own.

What he did appreciate, in reading the works of outstanding Earthian psychologists, was that they were pioneers in probing the human mind, that they dare to disagree with neurological concepts prevailing at the time. This, he felt, was a development perhaps not dissimilar to the sequelae of Darwinian theory of evolution. All these "theories", he thought, form a foundation on which one can build or remodel, a hypothetical basis for construction of more verifiable theories based on subsequent findings. Ookk thought with justification about the current turmoil in the science of psychology because certain facts were not known at the time of Freud or Jung. When science descends to submolecular and subatomic levels, psychology melds with neurology at the point when it is found that emotions are related to neural transmitters, that the speed of psychological reaction may be dependent on how fast the synapses, that are the junctions between nerve endings, transmit information at a time when they are affected by unrelated environmental influences.

The third line of thought which ran through Ookk's mind during his recovery period was the goals or objectives he should establish for himself and his future life. Basically, he had been brought up in a manufacturing society. The sub-martian space necessitated such a development. Limited resources and limited sunlight had constricted the

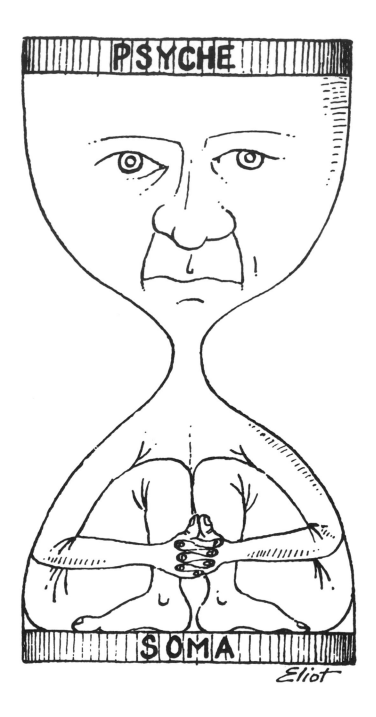

living space for Macrocells as well as for the giant Martians. However, while there were only a few hundred giant women Martians, there were hundreds of thousands of female Macrocells.

Manufacturing was all done in the huge cave-like spaces. This development was dictated by the giant Martians. "I have left Mars and I don't have to worry about the future of the matriarchal society", Ookk reassured himself.

Ookk's past, however, instilled in him the need to build, to create something. This is why he embraced rather willingly Mara's project of building a monument. He thought to himself that whether Mara deserved a monument or not was of secondary importance. What was significant to him was that something would be built, something permanent. Mara was his mother; without her direction, he would not be where he is now. She literally brought him down to Earth. The future was up to him. He realized, subconsciously, that to build a monument on earth to a completely unknown being was not realistic. His intelligence was telling him that if this idea could be converted or modified into a form that is practical, this could become for him a sensible goal. To have a goal was for Ookk a psychological necessity. The days of relative isolation from the rest of the group allowed him to dissect his thoughts and determine his future actions.

However, in spite of all these thoughts which crossed his mind because of the psychological problems which he expected, he remained confident.

***

CHAPTER 5

As THE days passed at the Prutenian Camp, Ookk was getting used to the Atlantan way of life: busy all the time with one thing or another, with little time to chat. Ookk, for the first time in his life, was in the constant company of three male Americans. Abercorn was almost always there helping the girls with installations and improvements. He became Ookk's constant companion, telling-him all he knew about the United States. He also wanted to make sure that when Ookk returned to Mars, his impression of this country would remain positive. Richard and Michael also visited the camp frequently coming with the Olympic bus. Ookk had a chance to ask all sorts of questions, including some personal ones. He learned that Abercorn was a widower – his wife had died of cancer – and that Michael and Richard were not married. He was anxious to know more about family life, which was non-existent on Mars, but the three of them were not much help in this respect.

"If I were you", said Abercorn, "I would not get married. If you do, you have to listen to somebody all your life, although, I must say, my late wife, Mathilda, was a good soul and we had a good marriage but, to be truthful, I was tired of her constant complaints that everything I did was not necessarily wrong, but that it was never perfect."

"So, why did you listen to her?" Ookk asked.

"It is a sort of a custom that the wife is the real boss, because she looks after the children and the man is supposed to be the provider. Anyhow, that's how it used to be. Things are changing now. My kids are grown up now and live in various areas of the United States. They visit me once in a while at Stone Mountain or at Christmas time, but mostly they just send me a Christmas card. They are too busy with their own lives and their own kids. They write more often when they need something. And 'so it goes', Vonnegut says in the movie/book 'Slaughterhouse Five'."

"Family life is changing. There are more single women because men die sooner, they get divorced or they simply prefer to live alone as single mothers. What results are 'single-parent families'. This affects the kids, you know."

"What leads to 'divorce'?" Ookk asked.

"Hard to say. I suppose if two people cannot live together, they separate. I am against it because, usually, they are not any better off. If they get married again, they don't necessarily do any better, and many of them divorce again! Don't get married unless you have to, son."

Michael and Richard were listening to this conversation between Ookk and Abercorn, when not attending to various camp duties in helping the girls. They had their own views on marriage, views of twenty-year-old guys, and they were not going to discuss them. They were interested in the girls, but not in marriage.

Abercorn was also trying to learn a bit more about Mars from Ookk.

"Do you have any plants on Mars? Do they grow as fast as ours? How good is the soil?"

Ookk answered these questions as well as he could, keeping in mind that he was not talking to a scientist.

"Yes, we have lots of plants", he commented. "Actually, we are all vegetarians because there are no animal species except the big Martians and the Macrocells. The soil is not very good so we have to fertilize it constantly. We also consume artificially prepared food because there is a shortage of natural foods – everything is rationed!"

During one of the following days, Abercorn went to Uta and proposed that he show them the Stone Mountain Park.

"I promised you I would; it would be a pity if you were to go back to Prutenia and not have really seen our Jewel of Georgia. I am sure that Ookk would also be interested. So I arranged for a tour with the permission of Mr. Brent Ericsson, the director of Stone Mountain Park. I told him that I wanted to show the Park to our Olympic guests."

They started the next morning by visiting the Coliseum – a huge entertainment facility – and the adjacent Sports Pavilion and Athletic Fields. Here were the archers, practising for the Olympics. Some of the girls from the team wanted to stay longer with them and help them to throw the arrows, but Uta rounded them up.

Everyone was interested in seeing the nearby Auto and Music Museum. Ookk was fascinated by the antique cars, and long conversations followed on the development of the modern automobile, a symbol of the American way of life. Abercorn explained how necessary and convenient it was on this continent to have transportation to go to work, school, or shopping.

"You are lucky", commented Ookk. On Mars, we mostly walk. The roads are of granite because the soil was stripped and moved to fields for cultivation of crops. At least when it rains there is no mud; the water is diverted from the flat-rock roads, which are higher than the fields. We have sophisticated vehicles but these are used to transport of manufactured goods and food."

"You must have very good shoes, if you walk on rock all the time!"

"Well", retorted Ookk, "most of you also walk on pavement. How often to you go the country and walk barefoot?"

"We have ADIDAS", answered Michael, "these used to be athletic shoes, but now everybody is wearing them."

The Prutenian girls were interested in music, the development of the gramophone and antique "listening" devices, as well as in the newest multimedia equipment, the NBC World News and, of course, all rock and roll recordings, starting with Elvis Presley.

To Ookk's ears, modern music sounded disharmonious, to say the least, and he preferred to listen to the classics.

"There is something timeless and soothing in the old music", he commented. "Maybe your new music portrays the problems you have, with its high pitch isolating the people from their environment."

The Prutenian girls, and Michael and Richard, disagreed. Tara, who wrote music, and Abercorn were on his side.

"I think they are crazy", commented Abercorn, "you cannot hear anything when they play their rock music and I think they will eventually go deaf if they continue to play such loud tunes."

"It is changing already", commented Uta, "people are listening more to country music instead of rock and roll; Michael Jackson and Madonna are now 'passé' in Prutenia."

"I think what we have here", interrupted Michael, "is mass psychosis. The entertainers get a crowd of several thousand people together and quite unavoidably, everybody reaches a high level of excitement. The response is mass psychology which is different from individual response.

Abercorn then led them along the old Hugh Howell Road, past the Ice Chalet Skating Rink, and the Fireside Pavilion to the Railroad Station, which for Abercorn, brought back memories of the railroad when it was used in mining and, later, in carving the giant statues on Stone Mountain. They boarded a train which took them around the mountain, passing the Memorial Depot, the Memorial Hall Museum, the Triangle Pavilion, the Brist Mill, the Fishing Hut, and the Children's Playground.

What impressed Ookk the the most on this trip was the Stone Mountain Confederate Memorial, the world's biggest natural bass relief carving, towering 400 feet above the ground and measuring some 90 feet tall and 200 feet in width. Everybody admired the riding Confederate Heroes, President Jefferson Davis and Generals Robert E. Lee and Stonewall Jackson.

"The figures are huge", commented Ookk, "they are almost as big as our giant Martians. Whose idea was it to carve the mountainside?"

That was all he had to say, the get Abercorn talking.

"I am not a guide but I happen to know quite a lot of the history concerning the carving. The person who first thought of it was Helen Plante, member of the Daughters of the Confederacy, who suggested it in 1909. But the man who picked up and promoted the idea was John Temple Graves, editor of a newspaper, the 'New York American'."

"But this was eighty years ago", said Uta, "did it take them such a long time to complete the carving?"

"Well, a well-known sculptor, Gutzon Borglum, began carving only in 1923, but they didn't have the equipment to drill into the rock. Borglum quit and the carving was taken up again by Augustus Lukeman in 1925 on a twelve-year contract; the drill at the time for hard granite rock was not good enough for prolonged drilling. To support the work, they minted Silver Half Dollar coins. If you find one today, it is worth a lot of money. To finish the story: the work began again on a continuous basis in 1958 when the Georgia Legislature established the Stone Mountain Memorial Association. They actually designed an esthetically satisfying portrait, using as an example Michelangelo's paintings. The work was done with a new tool, the thermo-jet torch, specially developed for granite carving. The work was continued under the direction of sculptor Walter Hancock, a great man who used Lukeman's design with some modifications. Ray Faulkner was one of the key carvers; he must have drilled thousands of holes in the six years of carving. This is the result."

While everybody was standing speechless, admiring the carving, Ookk's thoughts wandered to his own project of creating a monument to his mother. Should he start carving the other side of the mountain? "This carving has historical value. I must think of some other way of building a monument, something that would be useful now to Earthians and, perhaps, relevant to their current issues. I must ask Uta about the current problems on Earth."

He mumbled the words to himself, and Uta, standing next to him, overheard them.

"Oh", she said, "there are many problems on Earth; we can talk about it some other time."

When they later visited the "War in Georgia" Museum, the Prutenian girls realized that what was happening now in Bosnia had occurred in the United States almost one hundred and fifty years ago, except that the reason was different.

"The goal of the Union side in the Civil War", explained Michael to Ookk, "was to free the slaves, a valid reason. But to have religious wars in the civilized world at the end of the twentieth century is a crime against humanity – no excuses can be accepted."

There were so many things in the Stone Mountain Park that it was impossible to see them all in the short time they had. Abercorn showed them the golf courses and then they took the sky car to the top of the mountain, where they climbed the Observation Tower. The view was breathtaking; it was a clear day and they could see an area of about 40-50 miles all around, with he huge city of Atlanta to the east and in the other directions the countryside, dotted by houses and crisscrossed by highways and roads.

Everybody went back to the ground station by tram car, except Ookk. He insisted on walking down the trail. Naturally, Uta joined him and they met the group at the station. Abercorn was waiting for them anxiously, worrying that Ookk might get lost again.

The next trip they took was a cruise on the "Scarlet O'Hara" paddle boat on Stone Mountain Lake. The boat circled around the shore structures of Indian Island connected with a covered bridge, the Carillon and the various pavilions. It was the first time that Ookk had seen 'lake' water. He remembered their discussion about measuring the depth in fathoms of the Mississippi River called "Mark Twain". Naturally, the discussion progressed to the waters of sub-martian space. "Our water bodies are very deep, but there is soil on the bottom; as I mentioned, there are no animals, but an abundance of algae and other plants. There is also one huge sea, maybe the size of your Great Lakes."

"I read the book 'A Journey to the Centre of the Earth' by Jules Verne", interjected Richard. "He was an extraordinary French writer and visionary. He predicted the invention of rockets and many other things that happened after his death. In his book, he described a fictional subterranean space, devoid of sunlight, with a Central Sea and dinosaurs swimming in it. I wonder whether in his vision he might have seen the sub-martian space?"

"No Richard", replied Ookk, "the way you describe it, there was no sunlight in the Jules Verne description. As I mentioned, we do have a lot of direct solar radiation in the equatorian rift, which has an atmosphere similar to that on Earth; it is protected by an ozone layer below the Martian surface. What I was trying to convey to you is that there is a further sub-martian extension of our space into areas where there is no sunlight. This is where we built factories, mostly of granite blocks, because vegetable matter is saved for food. We developed systems which enable us to eat grass, because the fibre is broken down by enzymatic reactions. I believe your cows and horses utilize the same system. I will never forget the life I spent working in the cell culture factory lit by artificial light; no 'sol' or night, very monotonous."

"I forgot that you call 'day' 'sol' on Mars", interrupted Michael, "but you do have day and night and seasonal changes in Via Marinaris."

"Of course we do."

Everybody was dead tired at the end of the day, except Ookk. He seemed to have tremendous energy combined with the curiosity of a total stranger. He was absorbing everything that was said and asked questions constantly about the Park, some of which even Abercorn could not answer. When he saw a huge hawk flying over the lake, he asked wether that kind of bird lived on bones.

"On bones?", queried Maria, who was a medical student, "nobody can eat bones, our stomachs don't have enough acid to digest them."

"I must correct you", interjected Richard, "we have huge birds in Africa, called Kammergeiers, which have a very high level of stomach acid that dissolves bones. As a matter of fact, Kammergeiers live on bones of carcasses of animals!"

"Oh", said Ookk, I was wandering because our stomach acid level is higher than that of Earthians. We cannot digest bone, but high acidity is required for certain enzymes to break down synthetic fibres."

"On Earth", continued Maria, who wanted to show off her medical knowledge, "high acidity is related to a higher frequency of stomach ulcers; they may be caused by nervousness which stimulates secretion of stomach acid. Are you nervous?" she asked Ookk.

"Never", came back the reply, "if I were nervous or worried a lot, I would be dead by now. One gets used to trouble, to constant trouble; it just washes off you like rain and makes you cleaner and, maybe, more resistant."

As another busy day was ahead of them which included a trip to the Antebellum Plantation, Ookk was finally overruled when he wanted to continue the evening conversation.

They were up early in the morning and proceeded with Abercorn to a huge estate which, to Ookk, looked completely different from the rest of the park.

"This plantation", explained Abercorn, "was assembled here to show what life was like in the south prior to the Confederate War. Plantations were the most powerful economic institutions in the south which produced many of the nation's crops, mostly cotton. Plantations were owned by wealthy families and were operated by slaves. Not all slaves were treated badly", Abercorn emphasized. "On some of the plantations, they led the normal lives of labourers, which were not much different, let's say, than 18th- or 19th- century England or France. On some plantations, conditions were terrible, but so were they in England where people were hanged for stealing, and hanging was a public show on Sundays. The fact that the slaves were bought and sold was the main issue of the Civil War."

The group was first shown a large mansion, called "Dickey House" (named after the original owners) and furnished with original 18th-century furniture. Next was "Kingston House" which came from the Allen Plantation recalling the quarters of the overseer. The oldest house of the Plantation was "Thornton House" built in 1790 and transferred in its original state. Actually, the whole Antebellum Plantation was assembled from various locations, thanks to Mrs. Christie McWhorter, an expert in antiques. There were also the Slave Cabins moved from Covington, the Cookhouse, the Barn, the Cribs, the Smokehouse, the Doctor's Office, and the Country Store.

Ookk, as well as the Prutenian girls, couldn't take their eyes off the elaborate furnishings and the elegance of the wealthy homes, as contrasted with the stark simplicity of the slave cabins.

"There were also big contrasts in the way these people led their lives", commented Ookk.

"Such contrasts sill exist today on Earth", answered Nina, an architecture student. "People live according to their means and I am afraid it will always be that way. There is a lot of injustice on Earth, but different countries developed to a different degree and many are still underdeveloped."

"What I like about our country", said Michael, "is that if a person is willing to work hard and has the mental capacity to carry out the work he wishes to pursue, he can make constant progress and become wealthy."

"It is much more difficult to do this in Europe", answered Jana. "Children tend to follow their parents in the professions they choose. We have very few milkmen who become millionaires by selling real estate. We do not have the so-called "gasoline aristocracy". In India, it is almost impossible to break the caste system, and it is so in many other countries."

"To answer your question," said Ookk "as I told you, we have two classes: the working Macrocells and the ruling Martians. There is no possibility of change unless the Martians die out or accept our rule, when we refuse to be ruled. Then a caste system will probably form among the Macrocells, competing with each other, with their leaders fighting for hegemony. I am glad I am out of there and I am more than happy to be in the United States. If I cannot stay here, maybe they will accept me in Prutenia. In any case, I would be unique here, which I wasn't on Mars. There is not always a disadvantage in being different, sometimes it can be an advantage!"

CHAPTER 6

THE FOLLOWING night, after the conversation with Ookk and the discussion of Jules Verne's "A Journey to the Centre of the Earth", Uta had a vivid dream, it was so real that she seemed to talk to the persons and touch the objects she encountered. The dream was about Ookk taking her on a voyage to Mars, to see the world he had left behind.

Uta remembered quite vividly that after a long voyage, they landed on Phobos, one of the two Mars satellites, where Martians had a space station. The space vehicle actually descended below the surface and landed on a relatively flat surface shrouded in fog; she couldn't see anything outside, it was too misty. Several humanoids, dressed exactly like Ookk, entered the plane, which was connected with a corridor to another aircraft to which she and Ookk were transferred. They all talked some strange language but they also spoke English. They were all very friendly and delighted to meet Ookk and her. In her dream, one of them told

Uta about Mara's trip to Earth. Uta was also told that the purpose of the transfer to a special plane was to pass through a zone of extreme solar radiation around Mars, the same radiation that burned the surface of Mars millions of years ago. Ookk told her that the Martians considered it one of their greatest achievements to be able to pass through this zone around Mars. Had they not done that, they would be completely isolated. They wouldn't even know that the solar system existed. The plane which they entered was built entirely from titanium. Uta observed the crew of the plane in silence. They directed their aircraft towards the Martian equator and flew directly into the equatorial ditch, the Via Marinaris, a four-thousand-kilometre-long rift in the Martian surface.

"This is the entrance to the sub-martian space", explained Ookk, who was featured throughout her entire dream. "It's a pity that the Earthians could not pass through the solar radiation zone around Mars. Otherwise, they would know that there is life in the sub-martian space and that you can land there. We would have been in contact with Earthians perhaps for thousands of years! Professor Paul Davies of the University of Adelaide suggests that Mars might sustain life below its surface."

After their aircraft entered a wide valley, the strong blowing wind subsided considerably. They flew down further into the ditch until they reached a large, cavernous space which looked like a picture taken out of Verne's book, except that there was light. As soon as they landed, they were surrounded by numerous Macrocells who asked Ookk about his experience on Earth.

Uta was escorted from the plane into a huge granite building, where an equally large figure was sitting on a huge throne, with hundreds of Macrocells attending her! The scene reminded her of Gulliver's Travels, except that the giant was sitting.

"I am Mara", said the giant, "you are welcome here! You are the first Earthian to visit Mars. You can tell me more about Earth, if you wish. One thing I want to know is if Ookk has arranged for my monument to be built; I hope that it will be erected before I die."

Uta remembered what Ookk told her about his mother, and thus knew the correct answers.

"Your monument is going to be built in the city of Atlanta", Uta answered. "You have made an excellent site selection because the city will be visited by millions of people from all parts of the Earth right now. Everybody will know about you and will want to see your monument later!"

"That is excellent", replied Mara in a deep voice, which resounded throughout the building. "But are you sure that it is going to happen? Do you know the site?"

Uta did not know the site and had to think fast.

"Yes, the Olympic Park in Atlanta, or the Stone Mountain Park. In this way, after the Olympic Games are finished, the people can come and admire you. But the monument can't be built during the Games; we can only start after the Games are finished."

The giant seemed to be satisfied with her answers.

"Now, you can look around here and observe our way of life."

With these words, Uta was dismissed from the site and several Macrocells led her outside the building. There were all very friendly and told her not to be scared as long as she was among them.

"We will not lead you to see other Martians; they are jealous of Mara and make all of us work harder. Come and see our factories."

Uta was then led on a short tour of the sub-martian space.

"I want to see your cell culture factory", said Uta, "where Ookk was born. This is a great achievement that you did – to produce humanoid subjects!"

She was then led through a wide corridor into another valley where several granite buildings housed cell-culture facilities. The Macrocells demonstrated to Uta the process used in their cell-culture factories. The factories were divided into a primary plant area where embryonic clones were removed from other Macrocells, a sterile building area, an incubation department, a service and preparation laboratory, and a selection area of hybrid clones for use in cell culture. Basically, the cell culture technique was similar to that on Earth, with which she was vaguely familiar. She discovered that the missing part was the fertilization of eggs to produce both sexual forms.

The humanoid subjects were produced in the terminal facility. She saw some of them being born and put in incubators. There were crews of Macrocells working in each department. Special teams were assigned to the incubation department and the weaning department. From then on, other Macrocells took care of the children, which looked like those on earth except that they were taller and had more hair on their bodies.

Uta was then led to the synthetic food factory which for her was equally exciting. What amazed her was that this factory was really a biochemical factory where synthetic food was prepared from simple chemical compounds. Finally, she saw where the food balls that she had seen Ookk swallow were produced. She noticed that there were huge balls piled up, obviously intended for the giants, and minute balls obviously to be consumed by the Macrocells. She was told that photosynthetic food production formed a smaller portion of the process, because the space with the sunlit area was limited.

Liquid, she was told was water derived from melting ice on the Martian surface; it was stored in large synthetic containers and used for drinking, for use in cell cultures and the synthetic food factory. The water was crystal clear and, obviously, full of minerals. In her dream, Uta actually saw a waterfall cascading from the surface of Mars. Water was flowing, forming a stream emptying into a lake. Trees flourished around the edge of the lake which was surrounded by fields of fresh-smelling grass.

Uta wanted to see the communications factory. However, the Macrocell leading her on the tour said: "These factories are under the supervision of the other Martians. They even do not know that you are here. You see, Mara is the oldest among them, so she determines who supervises what. However, there are already some grumblings that she has amassed too much power."

Uta actually heard a strange thundering noise in the synthetic food factory when she entered. It came from a building where the Martians were overseeing the work. In her dream, she got scared and did not want to see anything more.

Uta was talking to herself in the dream. It became obvious to her that what Ookk had told her was true. Female Macrocells were everywhere doing all sorts of work under the constant eyes of the Giants.

In her dream, Uta then saw Ookk approaching her, his face lit with happiness.

"We can go back to Earth", he said.

Uta automatically followed his orders. They were led to the same plane that had brought them here. Soon, they took off to the surface of Mars and continued to the landing port of Phobos.

At this point, Uta was awakened by Jana.

"Uta", Jana said, "you are talking to yourself all the time. Some nonsense about being on Phobos and about going back to Earth."

"I am on Phobos with Ookk", answered Uta, "we are now boarding the spaceship to go back to Atlanta."

"You're crazy! You are in Atlanta!"

Finally, Uta opened her eyes. "Where is Ookk?", she asked.

"In his tent. Why?"

"Oh. I had a fantastic dream. It was so real! I was with Ookk inside Mars. I saw his mother and the cell-culture factory where he was born. It is amazing what they have there. But I don't think I would like to live there. It really looks like the story pictured in Jules Verne's book. I saw a lot of vegetation but no animals, except Macrocells and a giant who was Ookk's mother. I am sure that Ookk is right when he says that eventually the Macrocells will rule Mars. But when? In a thousand years? I don't think it will be that long. However, at present, they are completely subjugated by the Martians. They are really slave labourers. And they are not told all the secrets. One thing I wonder about is since Macrocells operate the communications factory which, by the way, I did not see in my dream, why don't they just take a spaceship and travel to Earth? I can't help wondering."

"I think that's easier said than done", answered Jana. "If it were possible, they would have done it. Remember that Ookk said that he is the first Macrocell to travel to Earth alone and that he is likely to be killed, whether he fulfils Mara's orders or not. That is why he does not want to go back to Mars. You see, the giants may suspect that Ookk is a man. Maybe this is why they sent him to Earth, to get rid of him. Where is he anyhow?"

It was early morning, and Jana and Uta proceeded to Ookk's tent. He was still asleep in his hammock. When he woke up, Uta related her dream to him in detail.

"I don't understand it", said Ookk, "what you have described to me sounds exactly like the place where I lived inside Mars!"

"I must have extrasensory perception, or is it premonition?" Uta surmised.

Jana was more realistic. "You were talking to Ookk yesterday and that was what you saw in your dream – a subterranean space."

"But it was not subterranean, it was sub-martian", insisted Uta. "Ookk confirmed that what I saw is identical to his space inside Mars!"

"Let's leave it as a dream", said Jana. "Do you know ABBA's song 'I had a dream'?"

***

CHAPTER 7

PRESSURE was building up within Ookk to take steps to promote the building of a monument to his mother. The Olympics were going to start in a few days and he was still in the Stone Mountain Park without having gone to Atlanta, his primary destination. Ookk felt confident that he should now move ahead towards his goal.

In the meantime, Uta also felt that she also should visit Atlanta and discuss with the Olympic Games Committee the question of the participation of her team in the competition. It was obvious to her that her team could not "jump" right into the elaborate network of elimination games. What she was hoping for was that they could compete with some college soccer team or play an exhibition game; that would fulfil her objective of promoting the presence of Prutenia on the international scene. She knew that one of the difficulties was that soccer competitions were scheduled by the International Soccer Federation (FIFA), while the overall planning and integration was decided by the International Olympic Committee.

Ookk discussed his plan of action with Uta since it had become pressing that something be done now. The action would have to be sufficiently dramatic to draw the attention of all the delegates to the national governing bodies. Uta suggested that she should fly with Ookk in his plane to the Olympic Village. The Georgia Tech grounds were sufficiently large for any crowd, and the Olympic Village was located next to it. Uta knew from Michael that FIFA was officiating in Athens. That would have to be another trip. She thought that the Olympic Committee was meeting at the Hilton Hotel, but the area next to the hotel did not seem suitable for landing. While Ookk and Uta would go by plane, the rest of the team would go by Olympic Bus. A meeting was held to iron out the details of the trip. Michael and Richard, their "umbilical cord" to the Olympic activities, were also present.

When Uta outlined her plan, Richard voiced the opinion that they should go by MARTA rather than the Olympic bus.

"You know, girls", he said, "if you show up in the Olympic bus, they may take it away from you and use it for some other team. When we go with Michael to report to the Atlanta Organizing Committee for Olympic Games, we usually go early in the morning when the big bosses are still asleep. David, your friend, authorizes the use of the Olympic bus."

"Who is MARTA?", asked Jana. "What do you mean to go by MARTA?"

Richard laughed. "It's not a person; MARTA stands for Metropolitan Atlanta Rapid Transit Authority." Everybody laughed.

"Don't laugh", he said, "it is an excellent system. I could bring you with the Olympic bus to the end station and you could take a ride on MARTA, right to the Olympic Village Station, which is at Georgia Tech. If you miss it, you will be back at the Hartsfield Airport", he joked.

"We certainly don't want to do that", said Jana. So, we will go by MARTA, and Ookk with Uta, and Michael as a guide will fly with the Martian plane. Is that O.K.? We will have a chance to see Atlanta from the train and you will see it from the air!"

Michael was delighted to be selected as the passenger in Ookk's plane. They agreed to meet the rest of the team in front of the MARTA station at Georgia Tech.

An hour after the Olympic bus left, Ookk readied his aircraft and flew with his two passengers straight into the sky. The view of Stone Mountain Park, with its massive granite mountain in the middle, was breathtaking.

"There must be some mystery about this mountain that I do not understand", commented Ookk. "As soon as I leave it, I feel that I am leaving something sacred behind, something out of this world."

"Well", answered Michael, "the Cree Indians who lived here before the white man came thought of it as a temple. Apparently, ceremonial dances were performed on the top of the mountain, and all the 'bad people' were thrown down the stone wall, as their punishment."

"Possibly I feel this way", commented Ookk, "because I am myself an ethereal."

Soon, the plane was flying over Atlanta, a sprawling city with downtown skyscrapers, the Piedmont Park, the new Olympic Stadium, the State Capitol Building, and the churches. Ookk was overwhelmed. It was the first time that he had seen a big Earthian city.

"You should see New York from the air", Michael interrupted his pensive mood. "There is no end to the lights, especially when you fly over the city at night!"

"I already know that I prefer Atlanta. Atlanta was on my mind when I was taking off from New Mexico; isn't it wonderful that I am finally here?"

Uta was speechless during the flight. She was thinking what Ookk had said about the Stone Mountain and their mysterious meeting. "It is simply fate", she thought, "I wonder what the outcome will be."

Ookk landed his plane at the Georgia Tech grounds without any difficulty. As the aircraft descended into a clearing in front of the MARTA Station, they could already see the girls waiting outside, clearly visible in their green and white Prutenian soccer uniforms.

A group of onlookers surrounded the plane, but the Prutenian team members formed a sort of protective barrier around it to prevent any mishap. As Ookk, Uta and Michael deplaned, they were surrounded by a curious crowd. Most questions were about the plane.

"What is it? Not a helicopter? What is going on?"

There were many athletes from different countries and their curiosity was intense. Ookk looked imposing in his Prutenian uniform, because of his height. Most people thought that this was some sort of a stunt to conduct a show at the Olympic Stadium. Some people suggested that the plane would be supervising athletic competitions from the air to detect any irregularities.

Richard recognized his mother and his sister, Elizabeth, in the crowd, as well Nicolette Kost De Sevres and her parents. Other friends from Montreal were also with them. So was Margaret Schmidt, Mike's mother from El Paso.

"What are you doing here?", exclaimed Richard. "I thought you were coming to the Olympic Games. They have not started yet."

"We came earlier, to get good accommodation", answered Richard's mother. "I want to see the gymnastics!"

"Well, don't forget to come to Athens for the soccer finals! We got tickets for you", he reminded her.

This was a pleasant, although surprising, meeting. They were just as surprised as everybody else by Ookk's towering figure, his plane, and the fact that Michael had come in the plane.

Everyone wanted to inspect the aircraft, particularly the engineering students from Georgia Tech who were milling around. Michael took it upon himself to be the spokesman and, with great authority, explained the advantages of the VTOL and its possible use as an ambulance.

"You mean that if one of the athletes got injured, he could be flown directly from the spot to the hospital's emergency room?" someone asked.

That question got Michael started on a long speech, explaining how this type of plane has already "saved hundreds of lives" because there is no need to go to the airport, since it uses ordinary gasoline.

In the meantime, Uta, Jana, Richard and Ookk went to the headquarters of the Olympic Committee at the Hilton Hotel. Hundreds of officials and reporters were milling around and they were confronted by complete chaos. This was not surprising. It was simply too late to make any arrangements a few days prior to the start of the Games. And many people were trying to do just that. Uta probably would not have been able to see anybody, were it not for Ookk. His presence overpowered any obstacles.

"Tell the secretary that I want to see Señor Juan Samaranch, the President of the Olympic Committee." he said.

The secretary did not even dare to ask Ookk who he was. To her, he was obviously some sort of an official guard with an important message for the President.

"He is just taking a break from a meeting which will reconvene in ten minutes. Who, should I say, is asking to see him?"

"Just simply say 'Mister Ookk'."

They could see the President through the half-open door looking at Ookk. A friendly and congenial man, he came out to greet Ookk.

"I am sorry. I do not remember meeting you. If I had, I would remember because one cannot miss your height", he joked. "What can I do for you?"

Ookk was quick to answer, without involving Uta, Jana, or Richard.

"I have come here with a very important mission. We have here a Prutenian Soccer Team, which has not been assigned to any competition. Prutenia is a new country and it gained independence only last year."

The President did not want to get involved in any discussion but, typically, he made a decision.

"Well, if it's soccer, you will have to see my friend. Dr. Havelonge, President of the International Soccer Federation. He is officiating in Athens. Tell him I have referred you."

With these words, he shook hands with Ookk, Uta, and Jana and left. At that moment, a reporter snapped a picture of them and several others approached them, asking for explanations.

Ookk brushed them aside, partially physically, as they left the building.

Uta was delighted. "Whatever happens," she thought, "I now have a recommendation from the President of the International Olympic Committee to see the FIFA people. That is much more than I expected."

"Ookk", she exclaimed, you were fantastic! How did you know what to say?"

"I just used logic", he answered. "It's good to be concise and to the point, if you want answers from important people; they get restless if you give them a long speech."

They went back to the Olympic Village by MARTA and related the story to the rest of the Prutenian team. Everybody was thanking Ookk for his help and he acknowledged his contribution promptly.

"You see, one word from a Martian, means a lot", he joked.

Michael suggested that they go and see their friend, David, at the Atlanta Olympic Committee, which they did. He was there, behind the desk, the epitome of friendliness. Ookk stayed behind to avoid any questions as to his identity.

"Hi, David", intoned Michael as they entered his office. "Here are your friends from the Prutenian Soccer Team. They want to thank you for your help in letting them stay at the Stone Mountain Park."

Everyone appreciates being thanked and David was no exception.

"Oh, that was nothing, just a telephone call to Mr. Ericsson, a director of the park. How do you like it there?"

"It is fantastic", exclaimed Uta. "All the amenities at the Youth Camping Grounds are in place. We are having a great time seeing all the wonders of the park and practising soccer in the archers' field."

"Don't they shoot at you?" asked David.

"Oh, no! Our girls threw cupid arrows at their hearts", came back the reply amid much laughter.

"Well, if you need any more help, let me know", said David, and he waved goodbye to them. As it turned out later, these were memorable words. Michael, on purpose, did not bring up the question of the Olympic bus, nor was he asked about it. "It's always better to let the sleeping dog lie, rather than arouse its curiosity", he thought.

The team returned to their camp in excellent humour, and Ookk, Uta and Michael were already waiting for them after an uneventful flight back to the Stone Mountain Park. The plane was pushed into the bushes at the edge of the camp, and they started another bonfire, celebrating their trip and singing songs to the tune of Tania's accordion.

They had one more surprise visit that evening. Abercorn came over and told them that he had heard on the radio that a soccer team from Prutenia, a new European country, has demanded to the see the President of the International Olympic Games, and there is now a big discussion going on at the Executive level as to whether new countries can be admitted at this point.

As usual, the press exaggerated.

"Probably, tomorrow our picture will be in the newspapers", commented Richard.

"You mean my picture will be in an Atlanta newspaper?" Ookk queried. "That's excellent! I think that I have finally made it!"

***

CHAPTER 8

THE DAYS were passing by and the Prutenian team did not receive any news from the Soccer Federation concerning the form of their participation in the Olympics. Uta realized that they could not participate in the officially scheduled games, but they did at least receive a referral to FIFA from President Samaranch. Tension was building in the camp as to where and when they would play, and Uta decided to call a meeting to form a plan of action concerning FIFA.

"We have to go to Athens and talk to them personally", she intoned as the meeting began, which also included Richard, Michael, Ookk, and Abercorn.

"Go to the top", suggested Abercorn, "that is what we did in Vietnam when we needed something. We bypassed all the damn hierarchy and went to the top general."

"It is easier said than done", commented Jana, "they may not even want to see us, when we don't have an appointment. These people are in constant meetings."

"I know what we can do", interrupted Ookk. "Why don't I fly you over in my plane. Everyone in impressed when someone comes by helicopter and my aircraft if even more impressive; you saw how much attention we received when we went to the Olympic Village. Richard can take the rest of you by the Olympic bus. You have helped me a lot, and I think that its the least I can do for you. However, I am running short of fuel; we will have to stop at a gas station. I saw one in Stone Mountain Park, past the Colliseum."

"Well", concluded Uta, "if that's the plan, let's get going. Abercorn, as usual, can keep an eye on our camp."

"You bet", said Abercorn.

With these words, they parted. Richard left with the team by bus and, after a while, Ookk, Uta and Michael readied the plane and drove on the road to the gas station.

"You should have seen the surprised look of the gas station owner and those around him, when Ookk taxied his plane for refuelling. Ookk's voice, as well as his stature, was so convincing that no questions were asked."

"Give me the best gas you have", said Ookk.

"Are you sure you want car gaoline for your plane?"

"I am quite sure; it is an experimental plane but it works."

They all stared up at the sky when the aircraft departed from the station straight up into the air.

After a short flight, they soon saw the city of Athens on the Oconee River, a small town surrounded by woods and agricultural land. They could see the huge Stadium, the

University of Georgia campus dominating the town, and some antebellum mansions. Michael, who knew Athens, explained to them the topography. "On the left is the Henry Lumpkin House, named after the father of the former Governer of Georgia, Wilson Lumpkin; further down, is the Lucy Cobb Institute, and the Taylor-Grady House, all built before the Confederate War. Athens was not destroyed like Atlanta, which was left in ashes. They joke that the double-barrelled cannon has defended it."

"The Butts-Mehre Hall, on the Campus, is the place where the International Soccer Federation meets. Should we not land in front of the building?" he asked.

"Good idea", replied Ookk, "there's enough room on the front lawn."

The Olympic bus with the Prutenian team was waiting at the gates and, as soon as they saw the plane landing, they joined them near the entrance of the hall. The guards approached them, greatly concerned about the plane landing, which they thought was bringing some important officials to the meetings.

"Dr. Havelange and the Executive Committee are meeting in the Assembly Hall. Whom should I announce?"

"The Prutenian Soccer Delegation", answered Uta resolutely.

In the meantime, the whole Committee, hearing of the arrival of a plane, emerged from the building.

"So, you are the enterprising coach of the Prutenian team", said Dr. Joao Havelange, the Brazilian President of

FIFA, addressing Uta. "and you even got yourself an aircraft to come down here. We did receive your application and President de Samaranch telephoned me yesterday that he had referred you to us. Unfortunately, as you know, all the elimination games have taken place and I cannot possibly include you in any Olympic competitions. However, I recognize that your country obtained its autonomy only last year, and I appreciate the fact that you went to a lot of trouble to come to Athens. Your team seems to provide a lot of publicity to soccer, which is good for our sport. I don't have to convince you that I believe soccer is the best participation sport in the world", he laughed. "Equipment is not expensive and the game can be played anywhere, even in the most underdeveloped countries. The main point is that fans love it; they like the enthusiasm of the players."

"Thank you, Mr. President. I realize it is too late for our new country to be included in the Olympics. All we are asking is that we get a chance to play against another team; it does not have to be a country's team – it could be a college soccer team", answered Uta.

"You have just given me an idea. Let's go back into session and maybe your application can be decided upon today."

With these words, he went back into the building with the other members of FIFA, and left Uta and her team waiting on the lawn, where the guards and some onlooders were inspecting Ookk's plane, as well as Ookk. Among them, Uta and Jana noticed a familiar face, Dr. Kostek Konstant, the bright soccer coach with a difficult name: Pawlikaniec. He had trained their team for several years in Yugoslavia. So they were excited to see him.

"Hi, Kostek", exclaimed Uta, "what are you doing here?"

Kostek recognized her immediately, as well as some of the other girls, and they hugged one another, to the surprise of Ookk, Michael and Richard.

"Who is this guy?", asked Ookk.

"Oh, it's a long story. He is one of the best coaches in Europe. He trained our team in a new way of play, in which the team is on a constant forward motion; you have to have a good goalie to play this way, and we are lucky to have one", said Uta looking admiringly at Jana.

"Well, Kostek, what are you doing here?"

"I am strictly an observer on the Committee that deals with proposals to modify the rules of the game. The issues are only now coming to the surface. I has been ralized that unless we have more referees on the field, it will be very difficult to oversee the whole game. As you know, in hockey they have three referees – we have only one for a much bigger field!"

"Well, I remember that when you trained us in Prutenia we always had three referees – it worked very well. You also requested that players change when they get a yellow ticket. Players get very tired when running on the field for three periods – that slows the game down!" commented Uta.

"Exactly, and the public gets restless! No goals, no action!"

"I can see that you're still at it, fighting for better soccer!"

"I always will be", replied Kostek, "we want to remove violence from soccer. There is no reason for it. If a player gets brutal, his emotions transfer to the people who watch the game; that is one reason for soccer riots. By the way, what are you doing here?"

Uta told him the story of their team in Prutenia, how their region was the only one where there was no fighting in the former Yugoslavia; how the President of the autonomous Republic decided to send a team to the Olympic Games and paid for the return tickets.

"You cannot participate in the Games", commented Kostek.

"We hope to get permission to play an exhibition game. That would be something! Against an American College Soccer Team!"

"But they are very strong!"

"I know, but we have nothing to lose."

"That's right", replied Kostek, "I will come to your camp and practice with you to refresh your memory. Our meetings are almost finished. In any case, I don't have any other important functions to attend."

"That s a deal", explained Uta. "Come with us now! You will meet Ookk.

"I can't. Is he my competition in soccer coaching?"

"No. Come with us and Ookk will fly us over to the Stone Mountain Camp!"

Butts Mehre Hall, University of Georgia, Athens

"Do you have a plane? I cannot come now. But I see that you also have an Olympic bus. Why don't you send the bus out for me tomorrow? I am staying in one of those 'Bed and Breakfast' places in Athens. I'll give you the address."

"O.K." answered Uta, "I feel that God had a hand in getting us together. Your very presence will improve our play and it will certainly boost our morale!"

At this point, Dr. Havelange emerged from the building and approached Uta. He noticed Michael and Richard standing next to her, in the uniforms of the college soccer team, which they had put on for the occasion. That impressed Dr. Havelange. "This is a well-connected team", he thought, "our Olympic hosts are their friends."

"I have good news for you", he told Uta. "You will be able to play an exhibition game against a college soccer team, right here in Athens."

The Prutenian team members were overjoyed. They began waving and singing a Croatian party song. Richard and Michael joined in with "For He's a Jolly Good Fellow", and the mood of the celebration spread to the onlookers. Some of the Committee members, who came outside when they heard the singing, were curious to see what was going on.

Dr. Havelange could not possibly remember where Prutenia was, so he began asking the girls questions about their country, the place where they were staying, and so on.

"I promise to come and see your game", he said. "You've made it. Persistence is one of the greatest virtues",

108

he said, quoting Marcel Proust. "Before I go, I would like to see your plane."

With these words, he approached Ookk's plane, who explained to him how the Vertical Take-Off and Landing system worked without the helicopter blades. Soon Ookk, Uta and Michael boarded the aircraft and took off straight up into the sky to everyone's amazement.

At this point, Dr. Havelange noticed Dr. Konstant standing near him. "Kostek" as he is popularly known, had a chance to promote his views to the Chairman of FIFA, and he really appreciated it.

"We have many problems", answered Dr. Havelange. "We have to consider both professional and amateur sports, the rules of the game, and many other issues. Not everything can be done at once, but we are going in the right direction."

Richard and the rest of the Prutenian team stayed behind and the girls talked to their old friend "Kostek".

"You must come with us now", they insisted.

Kostek became hesitant. He really did not have much more to do in Athens. Needless to say, he was itching to coach his old team again. "These girls are really good players", he thought to himself.

"O.K.", he said finally. Why don't you take me by bus to my place and I will pack a few things. I don't have a car and I travel light."

They then took Dr. Konstant back to his place and while he was packing, Richard took them on a walking tour

City Hall of Athens

of downtown Athens and the North Campus of the University of Georgia. They went to the Welcome Centre on Dougherty Street where they were met by Muriel Pritchett of the Athens Convention Bureau; they also viewed the many old houses, of which Athens has an abundance.

Then they were off to Stone Mountain Park, bringing with them their prized possession, Dr. Kostek Konstant. Naturally, Ookk, Uta and Michael were already there. A question arose as to where Dr. Konstant would stay. There was no other place for him, except Ookk's tent. Ookk agreed gladly to share it with his new companion.

"He is from another European country", he thought, "and I am learning more and more about the people on Earth."

✦✦✦

Taylor-Grady Antebellum Mansion, Athens

CHAPTER 9

When the Prutenian team came back from Athens, bringing with them their old coach, Dr. Konstant, the activity during the following few days centred mainly on soccer practice. They knew that they would be playing an exhibition game; they now had a coach who was not only excellent, but who had trained them for a few years in Prutenia and, therefore, knew the team. Dr. Konstant adapted easily to their camp life. He became a steady companion of Ookk and, since Uta disclosed to him Ookk's identity as a Martian, he used every spare moment to talk to Ookk about life on Mars.

However, these moments were sparse as he concentrated wholeheartedly on coaching the soccer team. "Kostek", took the team every day to practice on the field at the archers' athletic facility; they were fortunate that they were assigned a separate area where one goal was installed at each end for real play. Naturally, all this was done with

Abercorn's help. Under the supervision of their coach, they made rapid progress in their preparation for the game. Kostek was relentless in pushing them ahead, as any good coach should do, and they didn't mind because they knew that it was necessary if they were to have any chance of standing up to the American College Team. Ookk went often to observe their practice and was thoroughly impressed with their performance and with the way that Kostek was coaching them.

However, he became preoccupied with his own project of building a monument to Mara. In a sense, he was sorry that Uta and the girls were now busy with soccer practice. "I guess everybody is concerned with their own affairs; the Olympics are starting soon and I might miss the chance to present my project." He knew that the idea of educating people about their problems was a sensible one, but he did not know how to combine it with his "monument" project. He did not know what were the important problems on Earth: his limited information came mostly from Michael and Richard, who were not involved in soccer practice. Ookk approached Michael one day for some answers: "Tell me, according to you, what are some of the important problems in the United States? What bothers you the most?"

"We have many," answered Michael, "but what do you mean by 'problems'? We have economic problems, social problems, and all sorts of 'vices'. Why are you asking me that?"

"Because I asked Uta this question and she said that she did not know very much about the problems in the United States. She is so busy with the soccer practice, that I can't get any advice from her. I cannot wait with my project. What do you think are the major social problems in America?"

"Well, I am not a sociologist, but I can name a few. For instance, alcoholism is a problem, particularly drunk driving. I know that drugs are also a problem, smoking is another, and certainly there are other 'vices' as I call them. Drugs, like marijuana, disintegrate our society."

Ookk was surprised by this answer, to say the least.

"I did not know that this was a big problem. Nobody I know seems to take drugs, or is an alcoholic. Well, Abercorn said that he likes beer."

"You see, Ookk", answered Michael, "athletes generally do not drink or take drugs. There are tests which show in the blood or urine whether an athlete takes any substance; if so, he or she is eliminated. This is now strictly supervised. Apart from this, sports are probably the best antidote against drugs; you cannot run or swim and be drugged", he joked.

"You're giving me an idea, Michael", answered Ookk pensively. If I build a monument, it should show people the adverse effects of drugs or alcohol; it should teach them how to avoid them – it should educate them."

"I've got it", he exclaimed suddenly, "the seed has been sown. People could perhaps go inside the monument and see the exhibits on these vices. Otherwise, the monument would stand as a sculpture in an esthetically satisfying form, but have no educational value."

"I don't get exactly what you mean," said Michael. "You would build a monument with exhibits inside? As you

115

may know, we have the Statue of Liberty in New York Harbour, but people just climb it for curiosity; there is nothing interesting inside. Well, it would be definitely unique if you had exhibits inside your monument, but you have to design a darn interesting structure for people to even go near it."

"They would," answered Ookk confidently. "It's the curiosity instinct that makes people do things. I will ask Uta about it tonight. You know, these Prutenian girls are from various professions: engineering, medicine, food technology, architecture, even music. We must ask them what they think about the idea."

That same evening, Ookk repeated to Uta his conversation with Michael. She responded enthusiastically. Ookk had only to suggest something to Uta to get her interested. She suggested a "brainstorming" session to toss ideas around. Dr. Konstant and Abercorn were invited to attend. Richard and Michael were also present. They were spending a lot of time at the camp, so much so, that Uta started to doubt that they were members of a soccer team. "If it were so, they wouldn't be here so much", she thought.

During one of their rainy days, the girls dug a circular ditch in the middle of the camp, using their old "girl guides" technique; one could sit on the outside perimeter and eat snacks on the inside perimeter. This is where Uta called the meetings to be held to discuss Ookk's proJect.

"Hi, everybody", she greeted them, "you all probably know that Ookk wants to build a monument to his mother, Mara, the Martian giant. He would like the monument to also serve a useful purpose. Michael gave him some suggestions this afternoon and he wants to discuss his ideas with us to get our thoughts on the subject; so far, everything is very vague."

Following her short speech, Ookk summarized his conversation with Michael. Everybody agreed that alcohol abuse is a problem around the world. The Prutenian girls did not know much about drugs.

"But smoking", said Maria, "is even more of a problem in Prutenia than in America. I guess people are more nervous in Europe about their future and that is why they smoke more."

"We had a lot of problems in Vietnam", Abercorn interjected, "and we have never recovered psychologically."

"We are all strangers in Atlanta, except Abercorn", Richard interrupted. But Abercorn lives at Stone Mountain, which may be nicer, but is not really in Atlanta", joked Richard. "How about getting some local people into our group? You remember David, the guy at the Olympic Committee who phoned Mr. Ericsson to get you a place to stay at the Park? He knows a lot of people and he is an engineering student. Perhaps he could build your monument." he continued to joke.

"Why don't you call him", said Richard, directing his question to Jana. Come with me to the nearest phone booth and we can do it together. A female voice is always more interesting to a man's ears."

While the rest of the group continued the discussion, Richard and Jana went to phone David.

"Hi, David", said Jana, "you probably don't remember me. I am a friend of Uta, with the Prutenian team at the

Stone Mountain Park. It's wonderful here! Why don't you come and visit us some time?"

"I certainly remember you", came back the reply. "It's nice of you to think of me, but it get's awfully busy here just before the start of the Olympics."

"Actually, I am calling you because we have a problem. Not a major one, but very important. It's a plan to build an Olympic monument in Atlanta."

"Monument? The Olympic monument is the stadium. I never heard of it. Our school of engineering at Georgia Tech would know about it."

"Well, that's why I am calling you", improvised Jana. "You should know about it."

"That's different! I am interested in any engineering project. When should I come? Tomorrow?", he joked.

"Yes", said Jana, to his surprise. "But we are all strangers here. Can you bring some local people?"

"The only people I can think of is Nancy Nolan, Jim Babcock and Bill Crane of the Atlanta Chamber of Commerce. They know all the right people in this town! Where should I meet you?"

Jana thought for a moment. She did not want to remind him of the Olympic bus, in case he requested to have it back.

"At the Wildlife Trails", she answered.

"Wildlife Trails? Are you getting 'animated' and 'wild'?" David joked.

Richard then took the phone: "No jokes, David. We are like tigers. All the girls are 'does' but have no 'dough' and we have no 'bucks'."

"Good, Richard! I know that you like to joke. I'll be there tomorrow and bring Nancy and Scott with me, if I can. Good that you called me before the Games start, because afterwards, it'll be murder. Let's make it eleven o'clock sharp at the Wildlife Trails!"

Jana and Richard returned to the group with the news, and repeated their conversation with David.

"What did you do!" Uta scared them, "You invited important people from Atlanta to discuss an engineering project? Where? We are not prepared!"

"But we will be", answered Abercorn. "I know Mr. Ericsson, the Director of the Park, and he can arrange a room for us at the Evergreen Convention Centre. They have a lot of meeting rooms. Count on me!"

Everybody applauded while Abercorn pondered how to take care of all the details. It was agreed that Michael would drive everyone by Olympic bus to the Convention Centre, while Richard and Jana wait for David at the entrance to the Wildlife Trails.

Uta told Ookk that he should present his monument project to the group tomorrow.

"It will be much better if you do it. I know you will have to improvise, but I think you will be good at it. Usually, nothing is decided at the initial meeting, but you may get some ideas. Michael will introduce you as an astronaut, which you are in a sense!"

"It is easier said than done, but I will try." With these words, they parted.

Ookk talked about his project in his tent with Kostek, the Polish coach, who was new to the proposal.

"One thing I can tell you is what I do when I have to start a new project. I just toss my ideas around in a confident manner; by the way, I am always confident that things will work out. Then I invite people to speak and, believe me, when they are faced with something new, they do talk; some invariably criticize the idea because it is new, others take it at face value; still others become enthusiastic. There are always three groups of responders."

Ookk could not sleep that night. He tossed around in his hammock and then went outside and walked around while trying to compose his speech.

"I have to be confident," he thought to himself, "there are sixteen people who I know and there will be three outsiders. Only the three don't know that I come from Mars. I must tell Michael not to disclose my identity to them. Otherwise, they will think I am crazy. What problems should I discuss? One is air travel, but I am sure this has already been discussed everywhere. Perhaps I should mention space travel, since I'm supposed to be an astronaut; but this is not a 'human' problem; it is interesting but not relevant to the subject. Perhaps I should mention radioactivity; Uta said that in Eastern Europe, there are some atomic reactors which could blow up at any time. Was Chernobyl the name? I will just ask them what the human problems are and ask them for their comments, before I give a long speech.

Michael is supposed to introduce me as a scientist from Texas."

He remembered Michael's words: "Don't mess with Texas – it's big."

"And I am also big", he continued in this line of thought, "the association is good. I must try to imitate a Texan accent. In a sense, I am a scientist; I worked on cell culture and I made the space voyage. It's too bad I can't tell them that! However, I am not stupid and I think I know more than most of these people. Except Uta!"

Every time he thought of Uta, his heart skipped a beat. "She's such a sweet big girl! And so stubborn! One day, we will come to blows about whose projects are more important!"

Ookk finally drifted into a deep REM sleep, obviously dreaming. Kostek was awakened by Ookk's talking in his sleep.

"Are you alright?" he asked. There was no answer.

**

CHAPTER 10

Early in the morning, Ookk went to see Uta and gave her the details of his planned speech. Fortunately, Michael came over with the Olympic bus, so the transportation to the Convention Centre was secured.

They all sat down for breakfast at the circular trench table in the camp. Michael reported that he would bring Richard, Helen Nolan and Bill Crane of the Atlanta Chamber of Commerce, and Muriel Pritchett of the Athens Bureau Convention, directly to the Evergreen Centre. Abercorn, who joined them at the table, said that he was successful in getting a nice meeting room and that Mr. Ericsson would join them for lunch at the Centre.

Ookk was both ecstatic and fearful. Ecstatic because it looked like he would have an important audience when he presented his ideas. Fearful because he was apprehensive about how he would be received. He looked extremely tall in his Prutenian soccer team uniform. So why would a man in such a uniform, supposedly from Texas, want to build a monument in Atlanta? All this had to be figured out within a few hours, before the outside guests arrived. By now, Dr. Konstant was also wearing Prutenian Soccer team uniform. The only three people not dressed in this attire were Richard and Michael, who their U.S. Soccer uniforms, and Abercorn, who was dressed in the attendant uniform of Stone Mountain Park.

"Listen, girls and boys", said Uta "We have a luncheon meeting at the Convention Centre with some outsiders who do not know Ookk's identity. We must keep it confidential for now! I suppose that eventually everything will be made public."

She then took Michael aside to convince him to introduce Ookk as a Texan.

"Michael, you must not divulge our secret. Otherwise, the whole project may collapse. As you know, Ookk is a Martian and we do not want to start a discussion about that at this time and create some doubts in their minds as to the validity of his project."

"Well", answered Mike, "I have some doubts myself, simply because his English is so good and he knows so much about the affairs on Earth. But if Sumita says he is a Martian, I have to believe her"; at this point, he looked at her with great affection.

"Whether you are convinced or not is of secondary importance at the moment", said Sumita. "Do you remember that, originally, you did not believe that we were from Prutenia?"

Michael, would not oppose anything Sumita told him, because they always preferred to agree with each other.

"There's a lot of land in Texas", he said, "I live in El Paso on the Mexican border. A lot of Mexicans come over every night and are returned; but not all are brought back to Mexico. There are numerous newcomers. For instance, Ookk could be from Beaumont or Houston, on the other side of Texas. Ookk could also be a Cree Indian, for that matter!"

Ookk was delighted that Michael agreed to present him at the meeting as a Texan from Beaumont. It was sort of a joke and when they told the decision to the rest of the team, everybody applauded.

"You will be proud to have me as a fellow Texan", said Ookk, but I must tell all of you about my project. You will hear about it later at the Convention Centre; I'll just give you a summary because what I will present at the table will be somewhat different."

"You see, before I left Mars, my mother Mara told me that I should build a monument on Earth to commemorate her voyage to Earth and to acquaint people on Earth with Mars. Atlanta was selected because of the forthcoming Olympic Games. Personally, I want to make sure that the monument will be useful on Earth. One idea that came to Michael's mind yesterday is that perhaps the building should hold exhibits about human problems, such as alcoholism, drug abuse, and so on; you will hear about it when I give my speech. At this point, I am asking you to keep my origin confidential. At the meeting, you will have to pretend that you are well acquainted with the project, and that you want to discuss it. If you have any ideas, please bring them up. New ideas are always welcome."

They had two more issues to discuss before meeting with the strangers. One was the matter of names. Even among themselves, they did not know each other's last name. However, that did not seem too difficult because in Atlanta, as Ookk noticed, people tended to get on a first-name basis quickly. The other issue was dress: when a group meets to discuss a serious project, they must be dressed appropriately, Richard and Michael brought their civilian clothes. Dr. Konstant looked very respectful in his light-grey summer suit. The big problem was Ookk. As a supposed Texas businessman interested in the post-Olympic development of Atlanta, he could not appear in the Prutenian Soccer uniform. There were no "tall men shops" around and probably they would not have had anything for a man over seven feet tall. Uta went on a search and found a pair of pants that could actually be cut to look like Bermuda shorts for Ookk. Maria, who was a good seamstress, used the cut-off pant legs to make a sort of cumberband for Ookk's waist. A colourful Texas-looking extra-large shirt was also available. All in all, Ookk had a respectable casual look about him which, considering the hot weather, was quite appropriate. Abercorn was asked to get dressed in his Sunday-best suit. The Prutenian team members put on their white jackets. Michael thought of one more person, an old acquaintance of his in Atlanta, Jay Greenspoon, a souvenir dealer. He phoned him and asked whether he would like to come to a luncheon at Stone Mountain Park. The elderly man was delighted to be invited and promised to drive up in his own car and bring with him Jim Babock of "Forward Atlanta" whom he knew.

When the group assembled at 10:30 a.m. for departure on the Olympic bus, they looked quite different in their civilian attire.

At 11:00 sharp, they arrived at the Evergreen Convention Centre. They were met by Mr. Ericsson, accompanied by Abercorn. The centre was indeed a magnificent meeting place. Mr. Ericsson showed them around: the outlay of the rooms, the reception area, and a magnificent garden with a view of Stone Mountain Lake.

Jay Greenspoon came alone soon after, David drove up bringing Nancy Nolan, Jim Babcock, Bill Crane, Muriel, and Richard. Michael parked the Olympic bus at the side entrance, but David noticed it.

"I wonder what the Olympic bus is doing here?", he asked.

"I don't know", said Mr. Ericsson, "there's a lot of traffic of 'Olympic People' as I call them."

Michael stayed mum and pretended not to hear the conversation. After all the introductions were made, a hearty lunch was served in the small dining room, just right for a group of twenty-five people. The service was superb. However, some confusion arose when Ookk was introduced. People had asked his first name. He had to think fast. He said that his first name was John, people called him Ookk in honour of his grandfather, who was a Cree Indian.

For the Prutenian girls, this was their first occasion to be entertained in America. Needless to say, they were delighted – the food was exceptionally good. Uta felt she should say something.

"I think, Mr. Ericsson, that we can recommend the Evergreen Convention Centre in Europe as an excellent place for future meetings."

"I would be delighted", he answered.

The drinks that were served were different varieties of Coca-Cola and Georgian Wines.

"We all drink Classic Coca-Cola in Atlanta", Nancy said approvingly. "This is a Coca-Cola city, since a local Atlanta apothecary, John Pemberton, created the recipe in 1878. What do you drink in your country?", she asked Uta.

"Also Coca-Cola", laughed Sumita, who was sitting nearby. "The preferred hard drink is Slivovitz; I hate it, it tastes like methylated alcohol."

"We are non-Alcoholics Anonymous", joked Jana, not knowing the meaning of the word, "because we are never drunk and remain anonymous."

"That is not the meaning of the word", objected Richard.

The group then proceeded to one of the many meeting rooms. It was decided that Michael would be the Chairman of the meeting, which he soon called to order. He introduced the guest speaker, who was, naturally, Ookk, and continued:

"Ladies and Gentlemen", he said, smiling, "I wish to introduce Uta, who will say, hopefully, only a few words, in order to present her team. We are pleased to have here one of the Olympic teams who have taken a great interest in

Atlanta; their team members are studying various subjects and all of them have found something of interest in Atlanta and, of course, in Stone Mountain Park, where they are staying."

Uta wanted to put a plug in for her team speaking slowly and with emphasis.

"We came here from Prutenia – our soccer team represents the whole country. You all know about the war in neighbouring Bosnia. We live not very far from there, but I want to let you know that Prutenia is very peaceful in spite of the fact that we have people of different ethnic origins and different religions living together. We are all Croatian citizens, but the region of Prutenia, with its capital of Dubrovnik, has been separated from the main country of Croatia because of Bosnian War."

"Let me introduce you to my team members. I am Uta, coach of the soccer team; next to me is Jana, captain and engineering student; then Sumita, studying physical education, who plays centre. Her left wing is Lydia, a biologist, and the right wing is Milica, a law student. The 'midi' are Wanda, a food technologist; Tara, a music student; and Tania, a psychologist. The defence consists of Helen, a nutritionist, Nina, who is in architecture and Maria, a medical student. Our famous goalie is Jana, an engineering student. We also have an environmentalist, Anna."

"I also want to use this occasion to thank all of you for your hospitality, particularly Mr. Ericsson, a director of Stone Mountain Park. Since our arrival in America, we have experienced only kindness and generosity, starting

129

with the welcome by the Olympic Committee of Atlanta at Hartsfield Airport. Prutenia is not a rich country but we pride ourselves in our achievements and our honesty as Prutenians. Soccer is our national sport and we are happy to represent Prutenia at the Olympics."

Everyone applauded enthusiastically especially the Prutenian team members.

Michael then proceeded to introduce the guest speaker:

"My fellow guests, I am proud to introduce my fellow Texan, John Ookk, a businessman who came to Atlanta to see the Olympic Centennial Games. In the meantime, he became interested in the post-Olympic development of Atlanta. He has a very unique project, which I am sure will be of great interest to our guests from Atlanta.

Ookk then took his place at the podium and began his speech as everyone listened attentively:

"Ladies and Gentlemen, as Michael mentioned to you, I am new to Atlanta and Stone Mountain Park. I must join Uta and thank all Georgians for their hospitality which has been extraordinary. We are on the eve of starting the Olympic Games, at which Atlanta will be able to demonstrate to the whole world its vitality, organization and hospitality. All Americans are expecting new records to be broken in Olympic sports: in each sector new ones are being added. We certainly wish the Prutenian Soccer Team well. I do not know how far they will get in their efforts to achieve success, but the very fact that they have been selected to represent Prutenia as the only sports team speaks well for their efforts. I am sure that, with their obvious determination they will go as far as they can. Certainly, these are talented amateur athletes, which bodes well for the future of the world's youth. The very fact that all nations can come together in a friendly, though competitive spirit, gives us hope that peace will eventually reign on Earth."

"I have come to Atlanta for the Games. I am a businessman and will not participate in the Games, although during my stay in Stone Mountain Park, the girls taught me some soccer. My trip to Atlanta was sponsored by my mother, Mara. I want to convey to you an idea for which I need your help. I thought that all of us should show our gratitude to our mothers, to whom we owe not only our existence but also our upbringing and education. I was thinking that Atlanta would be an excellent place to build a monument to all mothers, including my mother, because this is the city where people will continue to come to, after the Olympics. Atlanta is a great industrial centre and is the site of some of the nation's industries such as Coca-Cola, National Olympics Broadcasting, Southern Bell as well as many new industries that find Atlanta a suitable place to locate their plants, a fact which I am sure the Atlanta Chamber of Commerce welcomes to the city."

"As I was searching my mind for a suitable theme for the monument, I thought I should get some advice from young people. What should be the theme of the monument? Personally, I think it should deal with the problems that affect our youth, because mothers always worry about their children and want them to succeed. I declare this preliminary meeting open for discussion. Uta has kindly agreed to make notes of your suggestions and we will proceed from there. Perhaps, I should emphasize that any plans for such a monument would be implemented only after the Olympics, but perhaps the start of the Olympics may give impetus to this project."

After Ookk's speech, everyone applauded heartily. Uta and the girls, who knew his identity, were amazed how well he presented his project, without telling the rest where he came from. Nancy Nolan then thanked Ookk for thinking of Atlanta and assured him that he was most welcome. Michael once again took over as chair of the meeting.

"Please," Michael intoned, interrupting all conversations, "we are being asked two questions. First, what are the serious problems on Earth which confront our youth and, second, what form should the monument take? Just to start the discussion, I would like to mention one subject, namely sports. We are here at the Olympic Games. I think that everybody will agree that sports is probably the best defence against whatever problems we have. It is good for our health; it is good for friendship; it is good for the promotion of peace rather than violence and war. Apart from all this, if we take sports seriously we get so involved that we have no time to get into trouble." Everybody laughed at this point.

"Our mothers, as well as fathers, want us to get involved in sports rather than in some other pastime. So, may I suggest", continued Michael, "that sports be considered as one possible subject for this monument." Everybody applauded again. "Any other suggestions?" continued Michael.

"I think that one other problem that will be facing today's world is a nutrition shortage, unless new sources of food are developed", said Helen. "I am training as a nutritionist and I am aware of the tremendous progress made in producing crops using genetic engineering. However, the population of the world grows so rapidly that nothing seems to be sufficient. While the civilized world invents means of eating less in order to stay slim and healthy, the underdeveloped countries are starving. Just think of the recent conference on desertification in Africa and other places – lack of water seriously affects food production. Think also of the many diseases which are affected by malnutrition and require special diets. Think of Alzheimer's, diabetes, cancer."

"I just want to support Helen's suggestion that nutrition be identified as the most important problem facing the world", said Wanda, a food technologist. "I think we should have an interactive exhibit where people can count the calories they consume and measure the kilo/calories used in exercise."

"I think that everyone agrees that nutrition is one of the key problems in today's world. What do you think, Mr. Ookk?"

Ookk became speechless at this point. He could not tell them that they use some synthetic food on Mars and that their stomachs have shrunk as a result. When asked to comment he got around the question by saying that the development of new food sources should be a priority. He added, "I am not fat, as you can see, but I am tall and I need a lot of food", he concluded. Everybody laughed and applauded.

Human subjects could be literally put out to pasture
if they were provided with battery-operated digestion
tanks, containing bacteria and enzymes similar to
those used by ruminants. This would enable them to
digest various vegetation by selecting
the appropriate ingredients.

"I think that drugs are a big problem", said Tania. As a psychology student, I realize that they are addictive and that addictions are part of humanity. You can be addicted to food, which is called bulimia. But the big problem is addiction to hard drugs. It usually starts with smoking cigarettes, then marijuana, and then progresses to LSD and cocaine. Drug addiction is so common all over the world that unless something is done, children will be born to addictive mothers and will be defective in some way. Unless we educate the public and face the problem, the future of our generation will be bleak. Drugs are grown in many countries for profit and we have to convince these people to grow needed food crops rather than marijuana."

"Thank you, Tania, that is an excellent suggestion. So, we now have three themes. Anything else?", Michael asked.

"If you're going to talk about drugs, you should also mention alcohol", said Maria. "I am in medical research and I have worked on alcohol problems. This is also an addiction and is related not only to environment but also to genetic background. Children of alcoholic mothers or fathers are more likely to drink, particularly if the person experiences adverse conditions in his or her life, such as becoming depressed. Think of the damage that drunk drivers are doing. It was recently announced that mortality, due to diseases resulting from alcohol intake, had decreased; I think this may be because more alcoholics will kill themselves on the highways. I am not against having a glass of wine or beer to lift my spirits – I guess this is why they're called 'spirits' – but it is a question of self-control. Again, public education is important. I have a personal suggestion. Drunk drivers, on a second offence, should have their heads shaved; this would be a social punishment – nobody wants to work with a shaved head."

Everybody laughed and seemed to approve.

"That's a very drastic solution", said Michael. "It would definitely infringe on personal privacy, but it may be very effective. Perhaps we can suggest it to our legislators! What is worse? A few shaved heads or a few drunken drivers who can kill people on the road?"

"Now, we have four themes. Any more?"

"Don't you think that environmental protection is important?", said Anna, environmental sciences student. "Pollution is a big problem because it affects our health. The ozone layer is important and the release of fluorocarbons and other substances diminish the ozone layer. We are making progress after the Brazilian Conference on Environment; at least people realize the problem's existence but relatively little is being done because of bureaucratic entanglements and private interest groups. However, you cannot simply close factories, which would result in loss of jobs; people would then suffer from malnutrition in a 'clean-air' environment. You have to look at it both ways!"

"You make a very valid point, Anna, and you hit the nail on the head: the issue is environmental protection versus the economic prosperity. We now have five themes", said Michael. "Any more suggestions?"

"I am an engineer", said Jana, "and I keep thinking about radioactivity. I know that we need energy and there's a discussion going on in my country whether to build an

DECEIT

ALCOHOLISM

SMOKING

GLUTTONY

LUST

GREED

LAZINESS

Human vices according to Jerry Eliot

atomic plant. I also know that new atomic plants could be made completely safe. But there are two problems. What can we do with radioactive waste; where can we dispose of it – in the oceans or on earth? – and in whose backyard? The second problem is an old one, created by old atomic plants on the Chernobyl model. Eastern Europe is full of them. Furthermore, the defective plants are not being dismantled but keep on operating. I think you also have some 'oldies' in America, which should be isolated, if not dismantled!"

"That's a very good point, Jana", said Ookk, "I was thinking of that very subject myself."

"So, we have six themes for exhibits", continued Michael, "I am amazed by the response. Anything else?"

"I am a medical student", said Maria, "and I plan to specialize in neurology. As a whole, the brain governs all functions, such as neural communication as well as artificial intelligence – so many subjects! Such a theme could be combined in an exhibition on communications."

To everyone's surprise, Abercorn Smith, at this point, made a short speech: "You know, I was an officer in the Vietnam War. Do you know what our main problem was? Communication. Let's include the brain as a separate theme. I am not a brain surgeon", he quipped, "so if you have any problems in this area, don't ask me for help!"

Everyone laughed because it was a good joke and he meant well.

"I wish to second Mr. Smith's motion. Communication is a problem everywhere and it is governed by the brain", commented Jay Greenspoon.

It was getting late in the evening. Ookk thanked everyone for their suggestions and they all thanked him for his idea of a monument to all mothers. "But may I ask that we continue this discussion? I need some practical advice as to how to go about beginning it," concluded Ookk.

Mr. Ericsson came to his help. "If our out-of-town guests have time tomorrow, I could arrange for a few beds at the Convention Centre. The soccer team is staying in their camp. I am very interested in this subject. If Atlanta cannot find a place for such a monument, perhaps we can build it in Stone Mountain Park. I don't mean to carve it out on the side of the mountain", he joked, "I hope you have all seen the wonderful historic carvings we have. However, the manner in which the exhibits will be shown could also be very entertaining. For instance, one could open a station for shaving heads of drunk drivers."

"This is the best idea I have heard tonight", commented Dr. Konstant.

"And now", continued Mr. Ericsson, "I want to invite everybody for a dinner at the Convention Centre. Perhaps you could promote our Centre when you return to Europe."

Everyone agreed and they proceeded to the dining room for a glass of good Georgian wine, after all this talk about alcoholism. Fortunately, true sports people do not drink excessively and no one ended up getting his head shaved.

"We are not against alcohol – we are against excessive drinking," repeated Tania, a psychologist.

After an excellent dinner, the people from the Atlanta Chamber of Commerce, as well as Jay and David, stayed at the Convention Centre and had a serious talk with Mr. Ericsson about the monument to all mothers. Richard was thinking at that time of his mother and was anxious to tell his mom about Mara's son.

The next morning, everyone felt refreshed after a good night's sleep. The Prutenian team went back to the Convention Centre and Richard again hid the bus, this time much further behind the building, to keep it out of David's sight. The Atlanta people were so impressed with the facilities of the Evergreen Convention Centre that they promised Mr. Ericsson that they would sponsor more conventions in this complex. The people who were the most impressed were the Europeans. They admired the large meeting rooms, the excellent food service, and the complete hotel accommodation with 249 guest rooms. All this in the middle of a large nature park and entertainment area with boating, mountain climbing and golf.

After breakfast, the group assembled once again in one of the smaller conference rooms, under the continued chairmanship of Michael Schmidt.

Michael began the meeting with a short summary of the previous day's proceedings.

"Yesterday, we received seven proposals for exhibits on human problems, in response to Mr. Ookk's idea of building a facility that would be called a 'Monument to all Mothers'. I did not expect such a fantastic response but we have two advantages in this group. One is that we are all young and our brains are not loaded down with old-fashioned ideas, and that makes things move much faster. The second advantage is that we are emotionally committed to the problems of our generation. We don't give a damn, pardon the expression, who carries out the project, but we know that something should be done. Atlanta is as good a place as any."

"Better!" exclaimed Nancy Nolan at this point.

"I agree that it is better", continued Michael, "I read in recent magazines, i.e. Fortune, World Trade and The Entrepreneur, that Atlanta is among the top cities in the U.S. for business and Atlanta needs business. It rose from the ashes of the Civil War and it should continue to flourish."

"I may sound like an advertising man for Atlanta", continued Michael, "but I am impartial because like Mr. Ookk, I am from Texas. I could promote El Paso. However, I fell in love with Atlanta while staying here; by the way, I also love Athens, a city nearby, where the Soccer Olympics are being played."

Everyone applauded Michael's speech. He then passed the chair to Ookk.

"I don't know how I can thank all of you for yesterday's contributions. Uta took careful notes of everything that was discussed. We are lucky that we have so many representatives of different professions, from music to medicine, all of which have contributed something. After the dinner yesterday, I spoke with Abercorn and he told me that the idea to construct a plantation exhibit at Stone Mountain Park came from the movie 'Gone With the Wind'.

People saw the old colonial setting at Tara and that reminded them that this was something worthwhile to preserve for posterity, so they built the 'Antebellum Plantation'."

I was named after Tara", interrupted the music student from Prutenia.

"You see, how word gets around" replied Ookk. "Perhaps, since my mother's name is Mara, we should use it as a symbolic word to start a project entitled "The Monument to all Mothers" as 'Tara' was for the Antebellum Plantation. In this case, the building should be in the form of a human body."

Everyone was startled by his suggestion, virtually disbelieving what he said but Jana, an engineering student, came to his rescue.

"I think that from a technical viewpoint, this is possible. Airplanes with "curved lines" are designed from computer models. You simply divide the areas into triangle plates which, when the surface is large, emerge as curved lines."

David supported her contention.

"If the Tower of Pisa were built today, we would not place less foundation on one side. We simply would design a "leaning building". Many structures are built in such a way."

Nina, the architecture student, was all for it.

It would be fantastic to have a building in the form of a human body. It would be unique from an aesthetic viewpoint.

It would also be psychologically "healthy" for people to go inside the body, to face and study their problems, our problems. A building of this form would also give psychological support to the idea."

The biggest support for a building of such type came from Nancy Nolan, the senior project coordinator for the Atlanta Chamber of Commerce.

"If you build such a structure, it would be a tremendous attraction for tourists, in addition to its educational value. We are already working on plans for post-Olympic development. For instance, how to utilize the Olympic Stadium. One area that I have in mind as a possible site for the "Monument to All Mothers" would be the Olympic Park; there are 23 acres of park land in the middle of Atlanta. Masses of tourists would go through there, just to see what is inside. Another possible site would be the Piedmont Park."

"You know", commented Mr. Ericsson, "even with all the entertainment that we have, we nevertheless learn so little from it. I think that entertainment should be combined with education, with learning; this is what I am trying to do at Stone Mountain Park."

"One other location that should be considered is Athens should it not be possible to do in Atlanta because land is expensive", suggested Muriel. "I am partial to Athens, an old city close to Atlanta. I call it the 'Soccer Capital' of the U.S.A., because of the Olympics. They already have a large stadium which holds 80,000 visitors."

The girls from the Prutenian soccer team applauded her loudly but everybody else said that Atlanta should be given priority.

At this point, Richard, who was sitting next to Jana took the floor.

"You know what, you say that you want to erect a building in the form of a human body. I know of such a form which was never built. It was in Montreal, when I was a child. It was designed by students at the Universite de Montreal, under the supervision of a sculptor, I think Pierre Grange was his name."

Everybody listened carefully and questions followed.

"Where are the plans?"

"Why was it not built?

"Well", replied Richard, "human nature is the reason. It was too 'avant garde'. It was designed for the Buckminster Fuller Dome, one would think a perfect location. However, at that time the people did not grasp the meaning of the form. Anyhow, the project with an exhibit on nutrition inside the building was never realized."

"But who has the plan?" Ookk repeated the question.

"The only location I can think of is the Armed Forces Museum in Washington. I remember going to Washington with my father and seeing a model of a human body at this museum. I think the name of the doctor who had it was Dr. Micozzi, he worked on fat absorption in cancer research." I don't know if he is still there."

"Let's get the plans", sounded the voices, "if he is not there, they can trace the plans through their communication network for museums."

At this point, Mr. Ericsson dashed out of the room, found the fax number for the institution in Washington (it was at the former Armed Forces Institute of Pathology) and sent a fax requesting information on the subject. To everyone's surprise, while they were still talking about the project he came back with two photographs: one of the model itself placed on a base building and a second one of the building in the form of a human body, positioned on the table, being examined by scientists at the museum. As the pictures were passed around, everybody was startled by the idea but pleasantly surprised at the effect the sculpture created.

The figure-building was sitting on an oval base consisting of two levels: the upper level supported the head and the lower level, the body.

Nina, David and Jana, being professionals, immediately grasped the meaning of the building but everybody else was also favourably impressed.

"The base structure could be used for commercial purposes", commented David, "and the building for the exhibits. The trick would be how to take people first to the exhibits to be educated and entertained, and then let them go to the commercial exhibits."

"That can be done by appropriate elevators", said Jana. "First up, to the top, the brain exhibit in the head," she quipped, "and then down, through the body, to the business base."

Scientists at the National Museum of Health and Medicine examine a model of a building in the form of a human body. Left to right: Drs. K. Loughrey, S.C. Skoryna and M.S. Micozzi.

"That could be a living museum", interjected Tania, "if you change the exhibits frequently."

"Why do you say 'living'," Mr. Ericsson wondered.

"Because the old museums are stationary, except for some art galleries which change their exhibits. How many times can you see the same thing? It can get boring", said Tania, who was familiar with museology.

The field of science is changing so fast," commented Maria, "that one can have new things in a museum every year or sometimes every month. For instance, they now have a new method for bone repair, a paste of calcium phosphate which helps in healing fractures; how many people know about it? They also have a way to by-pass damaged neurons in the brain by getting into the algorhythm of dyslectics, this was shown by Tallal and Merzenich who have increased the intersound interval between vowels. You can also have a mannequin telling us how fast alcohol is absorbed by the intestine and your liver enzymes could be determined on site."

"I didn't know about all that", said Jay.

"Very few people know about it, and even doctors are baffled because science constantly presents new facts", concluded Jim Babcock.

"What one learns in the textbooks becomes obsolete after a few years", Tara commented, "at least in museology."

"In medicine, they used to teach students medicine, surgery, and gynecology. Now they teach them according to systems: physiology, anatomy, medicine, surgery of the

147

Computerized model of the Monument to all mothers

nervous system, of the digestive system, and so on. Change is based on experience; there is constant progress", Maria concluded.

After all these comments, the meeting was adjourned. One final point was made by Ookk.

"If we get the model, what would be the next step of our plan?"

"I know", answered David. "We have a group at Georgia Tech dealing with visual reality. I can introduce you to them. Come and talk to them; they can make divisions inside the building on a computer. They have to do this sort of thing, with the hope that their plans materialize."

Ookk was more than happy. At least, he thought, the key objective of this group had switched from soccer to his plan for a building that would demonstrate human problems.

"It's good to win a soccer game", he mused, "but perhaps it is more important to deal with our social problems. I can promote my friends from Prutenia at the same time."

***

CHAPTER 11

$\mathbf{O}$OKK was exuberant with the result of the discussions that took place at the Evergreen Convention Centre of the Stone Mountain Park. At least he now had a clear understanding of the key problems on Earth, and of how the "learning exhibits" could be incorporated into his plan to build a monument to his mother – now to all mothers. This, he thought, would have general appeal; and people will see what they do to themselves and how to correct their problems. He particularly liked Michael's suggestion that sports provide the best and possibly the only alternative to addiction because they are much more interesting. "The nutrition exhibit will go well with the sports theme because it is so important to sports," he thought, "particularly participation sports such as soccer."

He remembered that David had mentioned yesterday that he would contact the people at Georgia Tech who could make it possible to see the exterior and interior of any structure prior to building it.

At this point, the Olympic bus had just arrived at the camp, driven by Richard, to take the girls and Kostek to soccer practice on a different field. There they would have a chance to play against an amateur team from a neighbouring community.

"Ookk", said Richard, "David phoned me this morning and said he made an appointment for you with somebody called Tolek, who is a leader of the Virtual Reality Group at Georgia Tech. I have to go with the girls to their practice, but maybe Michael can accompany you by MARTA?"

Ookk was visibly disappointed that Uta could not go with him. "Conflict of interest", he thought to himself. There will be many moments like this. She has to go with her team to practice soccer. The Olympics are starting to-morrow." He decided to wear his newly made civilian clothes, feeling they were more appropriate for the meeting.

"I can go with Michael by MARTA", he replied. "He seems to be my guide, now that I am a fellow Texan", he quipped.

They took with them Uta's notes from yesterday's meeting and photographs of the "faxes" from Washington. On the way, Ookk had to sit all the way to Georgia Tech Station because in the standing position his head touched the holding rail, which was very uncomfortable. Because of his height everybody looked at him as he discussed the presentation of their projet with Mike. Michael located the building where the Virtual Reality Group was located without great difficulty.

On the second floor, they were shown to a room, cluttered with plans and papers, and Tolek, the architect whom they were supposed to see, was sitting among them. He greeted them in a friendly way, and asked them to sit down, and started to talk slowly:

"David told me that you wanted to see me about a post-Olympic project. I must warn you that I am a very busy man. We are still working on modifications of the Olympic projects to use them efficiently afterwards. Don't you think it is too early?"

"I know you are busy. If you need something, ask a busy person", Michael retorted. "We have a major project on our hands: a monument to all mothers! But before I explain it, could you tell us what Virtual Reality is?"

"Many things! People frequently misinterpret the meaning of the word. My definition is that, in a sense, it is an inter-active three-dimensional theatre. The key components are a first person perspective and the ability to manipulate objects that you see; both these components are important. The fact that you see an object means that it is projected in your mind; in reality it is on the computer screen. For instance, you can virtually walk into a building and examine all the rooms as if they were actually there."

"This is fantastic", exclaimed Ookk. "This is what we need for my project. We want to see in advance what it will look like and examine all the alternate designs before we build it! Can you give us an example of how virtual reality works?"

Tolck was getting more interested in this strange character, not only because of his height.

"Certainly. I can give you an example, using extra-terrestrial space, so you will understand the principle."

Ookk paled at this point, thinking that David might have told Tolek that he was from Mars. But that did not seem to be the case.

"For instance, NASA plans to build a space station called FREEDOM. It would be difficult to study the prerequisites "in space". This would require a complete laboratory with a centre for astronauts and probably also for Russian cosmonauts. All the equipment has to be tested at zero-gravity. We can do the whole thing much cheaper – create a 'virtual environment' – a space station with all its associated components; then we create a running simulation of the FREEDOM station and observe it. We can look at the object from any position, any angle. We can enter the 'space station', inspect it, and correct any design flaws."

"This is indeed something we may need in order to see how our project can work," said Ookk. "I am actually from Texas and I plan to work with the local authorities in Atlanta to build an exhibit building, after the Olympics. As you know, people are concerned how to maintain the level of activity in Atlanta."

"I know this is a major problem", replied Tolek, "but let me speak. It is important to stress that manipulation of the scene be in the real time. In this way, we have the feeling that we are entering the real world."

"What are the current uses of virtual reality?"

"The greatest use is in architecture. There are many other uses. Brain surgeons use it to remove tumors. Students, like biology students who can practice dissection of frogs; it is also used for tele-conferences at meetings which people can't attend personally, and so on. All the possibilities have not yet been explored completely, but let's come back to your project. How can I help you?"

"I will make it very simple, Tolek. I have a model of a building in the form of a human body positioned on a base. It is going to be a huge building with interactive exhibits. Could you put this model into your computer, dissect it, inspect the proposed details and transfer the proposed plans into virtual reality? We are not quite finished with the interior plans but we have a good idea what the exhibits will be."

"That sounds very interesting," commented Tolek, "but it is a lot of work!"

"It does not have to be done immediately. What is of immediate importance is to project this building, or should I say, the model of this building in the Olympic Park. If we had a picture of the model inserted among the trees of the Olympic Park, it would give people an impression what it would look like when built. The best would be if we had a giant IMAX screen and project the building on it, but that is not possible to do under the present circumstances."

At this point, Ookk pulled out from his pocket a photograph of the model and showed it to Tolek.

Tolek admired it for a moment. "It will be difficult to build, I am warning you. All the lines are curved. I suppose you will build it from triangular plates?" he asked.

"Yes. It is a large building, sufficiently large to accommodate several horizontal platforms for exhibits. As you know, in large dimensions, the triangles will melt into a sloping line. This is very difficult, but anything difficult is also interesting. Show me the proposed exhibits and I will study them", Tolek concluded.

Ookk then explained the general plan of the proposed monument. "It would be a huge human figure in a reclining position placed on an oval, terraced building. The terraces would enable visitors to get close to that part of the building constructed in the form of a human body and, naturally, to take pictures of themselves. This would be much more interesting memento of the visit", thought Michael, "than peeking from the opening in the Statue of Liberty. There is really no possibility, either, of photographing yourself with the Eiffel Tower, because you cannot get the whole structure. Here you could at least get the whole head or the whole arm of the structure into the picture if you want to see your face. To get inside the figure, one would take an elevator to the upper terrace surrounding the head of the building in the form of a human body. The head would contain an exhibit on brain function and communication."

"From the upper terrace" continued Ookk "the visitors would enter the highest platform surrounding the body-form building, which would contain an exhibit on athletic activities, with all information available on an interactive basis. For instance, one might learn how many kilocalories are used per minute in swimming, running, tennis or sexual activity. The escalator to the next floor would show exhibits concerning nutrition, the type of foods one should eat, vitamins, minerals, and diseases associated with obesity or malnutrition. Another escalator would lead to the floor which would demonstrate environmental issues: pollution,

ozone depletion, deforestation, desertification, water preservation and purification, as well as personal oral hygiene.

A separate platform would deal with problems related to disposal of radioactive materials and development of atomic energy.

"Subsequent escalators would take you to the Alcoholics' Floor, where all problems related to alcoholism would be presented: drunk driving first of all, and also liver and brain damage from alcohol as well as the genetic inclination to drink excessively. The last floor would deal with drug problems, the means of fighting them and the effects on the brain and progeny. After all that, you would descend back to the base building. The front of this building would be occupied by a huge Imax screen with a virtual reality picture, showing all of the United States. The rest of the building would be occupied by conventional exhibits related to the industries of Atlanta. Atlanta is the centre of the "New South" industries such as NBC Olympic Broadcasting, CNN, Coca-Cola Centre, Southern Bell. Probably, in the future, also a centre for Georgian wines and a souvenir-manufacturing centre, if Jay Greenspoon succeeds in his plans. Since the base building will be occupied by commercial exhibits, this will pay for the upkeep of the exhibits."

"Before you go, can you give me some personal background?", Tolek inquired.

"Well", Ookk answered, "I am a businessman from Texas. This young fellow from El Paso is my guide. I am on a fact finding trip to see if it is feasible to build an interactive exhibit in Atlanta which would be architecturally

157

interesting and serve as a learning centre. I thought of Atlanta because of the Olympics and the vacuum that is usually left in the host city, after the 'show' is over. I think my model is unique and the people from the Atlanta Chamber of Commerce tell me that the project may be of interest to the city."

"Well, you have an ambitious plan! How do you get down from all these exhibits on human problems to reality? I suppose that this is the reason why this figure is reclining? Under the weight of all these problems?"

***

CHAPTER 12

FINALLY, the big day arrived, July 19th, the opening of the Centennial Olympic Games. Although Uta did not get any further news from the Olympic Committee, she decided that the Prutenian team should proceed to the Olympic Stadium, where the Olympic Parade was assembling.

This was certainly going to be a memorable day in the lives of the Prutenian Team: to represent their country the Olympic Games. Everyone was in a festive mood. They now donned their uniforms, with the white jackets bearing the emblem "Nunquam deficere", the Latin version of "Never resign". After a trip to the Stone Mountain Village Shop, naturally with Abercorn's help, they managed to buy white jackets for their coach, Kostek, and for Ookk. As usual, there was a problem finding a long-enough jacket for Ookk, but with so many willing seamstresses, they managed to lengthen the sleeves and the jacket as well. Due to his towering figure, Ookk looked more than respectable in this outfit.

Richard and Michael did not join them that morning, being involved in the Olympic parade, so the team had to take a ride to Atlanta's MARTA terminal station. Ookk was appointed flag bearer. The attendant at MARTA, was very cooperative in permitting Ookk to place the flagpole in the aisle along the seats.

Little did they know when they embarked on the trip that many surprises were in store for them. The girls were singing all the way and were admired for their enthusiasm by the people going to the parade. When they arrived at the Olympic Stadium, the parade was already forming, with the national teams being arranged in alphabetical order by country.

Uta automatically went to the spot under "P" and placed her small team between those of Portugal and Rwanda. Before the Portuguese delegation was the Polish team, and Kostek, who knew some of the people, went to chat with them. Naturally, Ookk drew everybody's attention, because of his height. Perhaps this was why an official supervising the order of the parade came to him – he probably just wanted to talk to this 'extra-tall man' – and asked him which team he was representing.

"Prutenia," Ookk answered proudly.

The official checked his papers thoroughly and then came back with an answer which surprised everyone. "I have here a note – 'Application from Prutenia approved' – but according to our regulations, the proper name for this country is 'Dalmatia'."

The Olympic Stadium, Atlanta

Uta and her team members were startled. Uta knew the name 'Dalmatia', as Prutenia used to be known, before it was conquered by Napoleon in 1809. She simply did not know that the Olympic Committee was so aware of their history. She certainly did not mind the correction as long as they could participate in the Olympic Parade.

"I am sure you won't mind if I transfer you to the "D" section so that everything is in order. I will need some documentation from you," added the official, "but let's make the transfer first."

He then led the team along the assembling lines and placed them under "D" between the teams of the Czech Republic and Denmark.

"Now", he said while he was joined by another higher-ranking Olympic official, "you must have a letter from the authorities stating that you represent your country. Other representations are much bigger – yours is only a soccer team – but it is not up to us to decide. Some countries have just three runners, while others compete in almost all the sports. Could you show me your credentials? I am sorry, but your application was so late that it was reviewed only here in Atlanta. We have nothing on file!"

Uta paled at this moment. She had a letter at the camp from the Governing Council of Prutenia, but she did not expect this course of events. She remained dauntless in the face of this crisis.

"But could we not show you the documents tomorrow?" she asked. "I will be late for the parade if I have to go back to our camp."

The Aquatic Stadium, Atlanta

"What do you mean by 'camp'?" Are you not staying at the Olympic Village?"

"No," answered Uta. "We are staying at Stone Mountain Park. It is some 15 miles from here!"

The official seemed to be agreeable and started to confer with his supervisor, who remained inflexible.

"I am sorry," he ruled, "unless you show me the document that designates you as delegates, you cannot take part in the parade."

Uta was on the verge of a nervous breakdown. "All this effort! And now to be rejected at the last moment", she thought. At this point, Ookk approached them.

"That is O.K., sir", he told the officials. "We will get the documents in time before the parade starts. I will go with this lady, if you permit the rest of the delegation to stay here and wait for us."

"That's O.K. with me", answered the Olympic Official. "But if you do not come back in time, I will have to remove them from the parade assembly."

With this decision being taken, Ookk handed the flag to Kostek and ran with Uta to the MARTA station. In a few minutes, they were at the end station where they, fortunately, caught the bus going to Athens via Stone Mountain Freeway. While on the bus, Uta explained the history of Prutenia to Ookk.

"You see, Ookk, when our country became autonomous because we were afraid of being attacked by the

Bosnian Serbs, it was named Prutenia, after a small river flowing near Dubrovnik, the main city. Fortunately, the Dinaric Alps separate us from Bosnia and Herzegovina. It was conquered by Rome in 34 B.C. and was called the Province of Illyricum, under Diocletian. Later it became a part of the Gothic Kingdom of Odoacer. Reconquered by Justinian, it became part of the Eastern Roman Empire. The Slavonic people, like myself, settled in the area in the seventh century and have lived there ever since, though we have had many different rulers – Romans, Venetians, Turks, Austrians, and Italians. France, under Napoleon, appointed a French General, the Duke of Dalmatia. Dubrovnik, a city of about 20,000 people, was founded in the 7th century. It has a palace, built in the 15th century, and a beautiful 17th-century cathedral. Dubrovnik is a resort and fishing town – that is where my family lives. Dalmatia was a great centre of art and literature in the Middle Ages. Perhaps because of this tradition we are all well educated."

"Naturally, I did not know all that", answered Ookk. "But getting back to our problem, we are just arriving at the Stone Mountain Park. Find the papers they're asking for. I think it's getting late and the only way we can be back on time is to fly."

"But how can we land in the Olympic Stadium?", Uta asked, not opposing the idea because she knew that otherwise they would miss the parade.

"There is enough room for my plane at the stadium," joked Ookk, happy that she had agreed to his suggestion.

Uta found the paper that stated that the Governing Council of Prutenia had appointed her as the head of the Prutenian Delegation.

Ookk quietly rolled the plane from under the bushes and flew to Atlanta. When they approached the Olympic Stadium, they saw the Olympic Parade just assembling for the march in front of the tribunes, where the important people were seated; thousands of visitors could be heard, high above the city.

Ookk landed the plane smoothly at the back of the Olympic field. Several Olympic officials ran towards them, asking for their landing permit, but Ookk brushed them aside, saying that he has important information for Count de Samaranch. They left the plane and dashed over to their team. Ookk took the flagpole from Kostek just as the parade began to move. The Olympic official who demanded the papers, was not anywhere in sight, but Uta had them in her hands, and when she met the other official she gave the papers to him.

The Prutenian team members could not help but chant when they approached the reviewing stand and, to their surprise, President of I.O.C. Samaranch, the Mayor of Atlanta Bill Campbell, and Dr. Havelonge, President of FIFA, waved to them.

The plane's landing created great excitement among the onlookers. Most of them thought that this was part of the show, and when they saw two tall figures running to the marching column everybody cheered loudly; only the Olympic Committee people knew that this was an unscheduled landing and wondered what the "helicopter" without blades was doing in the Olympic Stadium. Actually, after the parade, President Samaranch could not overcome his curiosity and, before the official reception, walked over to Ookk's plane with numerous officials following him. Ookk, Uta and the whole group was standing around with a crowd of onlookers from other teams. Among them was Richard, standing next to Jana, and Michael with Sumita.

I.O.C. President Samaranch approached Ookk.

"I think I met you at the Hilton Hotel headquarters when you came with your friends asking for permission for your team to participate in the Games."

"Your memory is perfect, Your Excellency", replied Ookk. "Thank you for recommending us to Dr. Havelonge. He arranged for our team to play an exhibition game against an American College Soccer Team."

"I am happy to hear that. If I have the time, I will come to watch the game. But, tell me, just to satisfy my curiosity, where did you grow so tall? You are probably the tallest athlete I have ever met!"

Ookk paled at this point. He saw no reason to lie. Everyone looked at him when he answered:

"Your Excellency, you may laugh, but I am from the planet Mars. I am not a real Martian, but a product of cell culture; I cannot explain at this time all the details of my arrival on Earth, but if you are interested, I will gladly meet you privately. You may think I am crazy, but I assure you that I am sound of mind."

President Samaranch, was astounded. But he was a man ready to believe anything that was presented to him in an orderly fashion.

"I am interested in your story," he answered. "I am extremely busy and I will be even busier as the Olympics unfold. We have more teams in Atlanta than we expected. Some people make last minute arrangements and expect that everything will fall into place. Why don't you come at 4 o'clock to the Hilton Hotel, pass the guards as you did the last time, and we can spend thirty minutes discussing this subject, which is of extreme interest to me."

He then deliberately changed the subject, addressing Uta: "I am sure you were surprised to hear that the proper name for Prutenia is Dalmatia. I live in Switzerland and I know European history quite well. I visited Dalmatia and Dubrovnik during the Olympic Games in Sarajevo. You have a beautiful country and some beautiful islands off shore. Best wishes for your game."

He then departed with the group of officials following him.

Some of the dignitaries including Bill Campbell, the Mayor of Atlanta, stayed behind and started to talk to the girls from Dalmatia.

"This is a fantastic plane that you have," asked the Mayor. "Tell me, did you invent the story for President Samaranch or is it true that you are from Mars?"

"It is true, your Honour," Uta answered for Ookk. "He is staying at our camp at Stone Mountain Park. We met him soon after he landed at the Wildlife Trails."

"That is a beautiful area," answered the Mayor omitting a comment, "Several of the athletic events, including archery and tennis, are taking place there. If I have time to attend them, I may visit you. I cannot promise but I would like to hear your fascinating story.

Many people admired Ookk's plane and word soon spread like wildfire that a man claiming to be a Martian was at the Olympics. Several reporters approached Ookk asking for interviews and taking pictures of him, Uta, and everybody else they could get a hold of. Ookk, however, refused any interviews.

"I cannot tell you anything before I speak to the Olympic officials. There will be a time when I will tell you the whole story. I may even write a book about it."

Ookk then switched the conversation to his aircraft, explaining its design and how he had come directly from Stone Mountain, without going to the airport.

Uta, Kostek, the Prutenian girls as well as Richard and Michael helped Ookk to answer, or better still, to ward off all the questions. They concentrated instead on describing the advantages of the plane.

It was early afternoon and Ookk remembered that he had an appointment at 4 o'clock with President Samaranch. He told Uta to stay at the site with her team and to watch his plane. They formed a cordon around it and kept busy describing the aircraft to the onlookers.

Ookk asked Richard to accompany him to the Hilton Hotel. Michael volunteered to come along to meet the President of the International Olympic Committee. They went by MARTA to downtown Atlanta. Ookk was admiring the tall buildings and the activity on the streets . Atlanta, on this day, was what could be described as an Olympic frenzy. People were streaming along the streets, buying souvenirs from numerous kiosks positioned on the streets. Soon they faced the guards at the Hilton Hotel. Ookk, with his now well-known nonchalance, walked past everybody, leading Richard and Michael like two kids. They were taken by escalator to the top floor where President Samaranch was resting in his quarters after a heavy day that had started with the meetings beginning at 6 A.M. He received them in the foyer, after Ookk had asked him whether Richard and Michael could be present.

"Your American friends are most welcome", he intoned. "At least I will have witnesses that I did not hold secret talks with you. That's what the newspapers would say. Tell me briefly your story again."

Ookk repeated the facts he had told Uta and the others about the giant Martians, the cataclysm on Mars that had decimated the population, and the sub-martian space where the Macrocells worked and lived with the remaining giant Martians.

At this point, the President directed his questions to Richard and Michael, but he did not want to appear disbelieving.

"How long have you known Ookk?"

"Two weeks", they replied simultaneously.

"And you believe that he is from Mars?"

"Actually, he came to Atlanta from New Mexico", answered Mike, "but he claims that the spacecraft that brought him from Mars did not remain on earth."

"If this is true, this will be the big story of the Olympics," answered the President. "What are your future plans?"

"I plan to build an educational facility in Atlanta, something that will leave a lasting memory of this Olympics", answered Ookk.

President de Samaranch became very pensive at this point.

"I think this is an excellent idea," he said. Some cities have problems as to what to do after the Olympics and how to go through the "post-partum" period. Why don't you talk to Bill Campbell? I am warning you that it will be very difficult to find money for a project like that!"

"Not the way I have planned it", said Ookk. "But I am very grateful that you have seen me. You are a great man!"

With these words, they left and returned to the Olympic stadium and Ookk's plane. There was still a crowd surrounding the aircraft, with many reporters who had heard about the events, just waiting for Ookk in order to take more pictures.

Ookk, Uta and Michael decided to leave immediately. While the girls formed a cordon around the plane, the aircraft took off straight up into the sky, to the bewilderment of the onlookers. The girls, with Richard and Kostek, went by ground transportation back to Stone Mountain Park, where Ookk was already waiting for them.

The team members brought with them some newspapers with pictures of Ookk, Uta, President Samaranch, Mayor Bill Campbell, and many other officials. They showed them the titles of the articles that were published: "Samaranch Meets a Martian"; "A Strange Man from Dalmatia Claims to Come from Another Planet"; "Possibility of Life on Mars Becomes Real"; and "Watch Your Step: The Martians are Coming."

Ookk was happy that everything had worked out in his favour and that his identity was now revealed. He had felt very uncomfortable pretending to be somebody else. By the disclosure his sense of self had been preserved. This is what he thought at that time!

***

CHAPTER 13

OOKK felt unequivocally successful after the days events at the Olympic Stadium. He met the President of the Olympic Games, as well as the Mayor of Atlanta, and he conveyed to them his plans to erect an educational building in the City after the Olympic Games were finished. In reality, nothing concrete had been done but the fact that he had been identified by very knowledgeable people as a key person in a major undertaking was for him psychologically important. What a difference to his previous life as a "number" working in a cell-culture factory, without the possibility of expressing any of his ideas, which were always unique and on a large scale. Perhaps the day of the opening of the Olympic Games had produced a major psychological transformation in his way of thinking. He now was capable of doing things and was confident that he could do them on his own.

The fallout from yesterday's events was tremendous. Abercorn, who, had come early to the Stone Mountain Park, reported that the landing of the plane at the Olympic Stadium was probably the best barometer of public reaction to the knowledge that a Martian was not only present in Atlanta but would possibly participate in the Olympic Games.

Everyone assembled in the camp for breakfast to hear his comments:

"You know, Ookk, you made quite an impression on the crowd when you landed your plane at the Stadium. And then, as everyone was watching, the Mayor of Atlanta and the fellow who is in charge of the Olympics went over to see you. I don't know what they said, I also heard that the International Olympic Committee invited you to talk to them at the Hilton Hotel headquarters in the afternoon."

"The newspapers made quite a story out of this. Some articles stated that you were going to bring Martians to the next Games. Since they are much bigger, all athletic records on Earth would be broken. That would not be fair to our people. Others claimed that you just came to see the conditions on Earth and to see whether life here was better than on Mars. Still others said that you were not from Mars and that the whole story was invented by the Olympic officials to promote the games."

"I've known you since you came here and I have no doubt about what you told us about living on Mars. I have told this to other people in the Park, who know that you are staying at the Youth Camping Grounds, and that I know you personally. They are very proud to have you here and at the Stone Mountain Village; they are saying that the fact that you are staying here will be good for tourism."

174

Ookk was happy with the news that Abercorn brought from the outside world. Nevertheless, he resented being thought of as a tourist attraction, as something unusual but of little value except for entertainment. Since there was no entertainment on Mars, he did not understand the value of entertainment as a psychological relaxant. But he wondered why a person who entertains all his life, feels like a cultural icon. He foresaw, following yesterday's events, that a new chapter was opening up in his life on Earth, that he might have an opportunity to realize his project of building a "Monument to All Mothers" as he now called it in his own mind. "The dice have been thrown", he thought, quoting Caesar, "it depends how I play the game. There will be many other obstacles and factors affecting the outcome, but at least I have a fair chance of going ahead with it."

At this point, the issue crucial to further developments was his relationship with Uta, or at least that's what he thought. She had helped him this far in all his undertakings on Earth; she looked after him, telling him about all the details of life on Earth and, literally, telling him what to do. He thought that he loved her, a feeling he had never experienced before; he was certain that she loved him, though they never kissed or had any romantic encounter. Since the Macrocells on Mars were raised as asexual females, they did not attract him; rather he felt antagonized by their indifference, not only to himself, but to other Macrocells as well. "They are simple robots," he thought, remembering his earlier life. "All they want is to get a better job so that their standard of living will be higher."

Ookk was torn between two feelings: he felt that he needed Uta to accompany him on his ventures to carry out

175

his project; yet on the other hand, he wanted to convince himself and others that he could do things on his own. The current state of affairs tended to promote his independence, since Uta was involved with the soccer practice. Her companion and "master" at the moment was the Polish coach, Kostek, who trained her team for the forthcoming exhibition game. Ookk found himself waiting for an opportunity to talk things over with her and to clarify some issues.

The opportunity came when Uta invited him for a walk after supper. The Park was alive with all sorts of festivities, such as laser shows on the north side of the mountain, and music from the Coliseum. There was a crowd walking in a festive mood on Robert Lee Boulevard. Ookk and Uta went to the Wildlife Trails, which was quiet as usual, but not deserted. The evening was pleasant, bright with stars, and a light wind cooling the hot day. They were holding hands when Uta started the conversation.

"Ookk, I worry about you. You might be disappointed if your project does not materialize. I know that you have made fantastic progress up to now but a lot is waiting for you."

"I, myself, have no doubt that I can succeed ", Ookk answered. "I am audacious enough to carry it through. I know that the newspapers made some unjustified statements, but this does not mean that I cannot do it. People don't know my potential. It's too bad that you cannot help me with this project at a time when I feel that it can really be realized."

Uta started to cry.

"Ookk," she said, "you know that I would do anything for you. And you must admit that I have already helped you a lot. But what do you want me to do? I have to practice soccer daily, otherwise we will have no chance of winning against the American soccer team. You don't really want me to stop practising. We came to Atlanta to play soccer."

"But, how about this fellow Kostek? He is now your master – you do everything he asks you to do. Do you really admire him?"

"I must admit I do, but I admire him as a coach. I wouldn't think of exchanging him for you!"

"Uta, do you think you own me? Why don't you admit that you admire Kostek as a man."

"There is nothing wrong with admiring Kostek as a man", she replied rather facetiously. "If it weren't for him, we would certainly lose the game for sure. I don't think I own you and you don't own me. Everybody owns him or herself and that's the way it should be. I know that most people are not autonomous and that they rely on someone else. But this is not healthy; who wants to rely on Freud? I would rather rely on what Jung says.

Uta's talk surprised Ookk. "I always knew that she was a very independent person", he thought, "but it's sort of selfish to want to win a game when there are other more important issues facing the world which I am trying to solve. On the other hand, who knows whether I can do anything, while she knows that she can probably win the damn game" (Ookk was learning how to swear, just by listening to Abercorn).

For a few moments, complete silence reigned between them as both were immersed in their own thoughts, wondering how their relationship would develop from now on. Finally, Ookk broke the silence.

"Uta, I think I should act on my own and go ahead with my plans, and that you should continue to practice soccer. It would be unfair of me to get you involved in a project which is so uncertain, and may cause you to forego your plans. We can still remain friends but, perhaps, we should not continue the sort of relationship that leads to a permanent tie. I don't know what I will do on Earth, although I know that I don't wish to go back to Mars, unless I am forced to return. You will probably go back to Prutenia or Dalmatia, whatever the name is, and be a hero there. It is your psychological make-up to be a winner and you should remain so!"

These words came as a blow to Uta. Because of the soccer game, she might be breaking her ties with a man who was her idol! She was sure that she loved him. But, now, to demand, more or less, that she cut down her preparation for what was probably the most crucial time in her career, was definitely asking too much. She suddenly realized that Ookk was probably jealous of Kostek. He mentioned something that alluded to this possibility. So she tried again:

"Ookk," she said, "there is nothing between Kostek and me. If that's your worry, just forget it!"

"No," Ookk replied, "what I am saying is that we have a conflict of interest situation. For me, the most important thing is to pursue my project. You realize that when the Olympics are finished, all these people will be gone. It's a 'now or never' situation!"

178

"Ookk, I am faced with the same situation. If our team loses the game badly to the Americans, let's say we don't score any goals and they score ten, we will be a laughing stock at home and at the Olympics. At home, they will say: 'we should never have collected the money to send them there; they have shown that our country cannot compete in any international games'. And in Atlanta, they will say that rules should be changed not to allow just anyone who wants to see Atlanta to receive royal treatment at the Olympic Games. But I must say that the people here are very friendly, and not necessarily for business reasons; that's why we feel welcome. But to finish our discussion, let's do what you suggested. You can pursue your project on your own, and I will lead the soccer practice. In any case, if one of us wins, it will be good for both of us, if we can trust one another, and I think we should."

After they returned to the camp, Ookk repeated his conversation with Uta to Kostek, and Uta repeated it to Jana. That is how "word" spreads around: one shares it with the person one is with at the time. Kostek assured Ookk that he was not in love with Uta, but that he admired her highly. He supported her unequivocally her intention to spend a lot of time preparing for the exhibition soccer match.

"You know," he told Ookk, "to win is also my ambition as well as of the whole team. Do you know what it means for a soccer coach to lose a crucial game? I would probably never get a job anywhere else. I know that everybody has good and bad days, but the public judges a coach by the way his team plays. I have taught them a new way of attack. We will also have three referees, because the linesmen cannot participate in judging to reduce the number of fouls.

The next day, Jana repeated the conversation between Ookk and Uta to Richard. That brought their relationship into focus. Richard was not busy so he did not mind that Jana spent her days practising as a goalie. As a matter of fact, he played occasionally with her, just shooting goals from different directions to test her skills and to give her advice. Richard wanted to tell her more about himself.

"You know that I am not a member of the American Soccer Team. I am only on a replacement team."

"Oh!" she answered, "I thought you were on the main team."

"Well, I didn't want to tell anyone but I want to tell you the truth. I am just out of high school and I concentrated on my studies. You know how tough it is to get on the National College Team! You have to practice at least for a year; to do that, I would have to drop out of college. I want to go to college this fall, so I could not afford it."

"What do you want to study?"

"Probably dental surgery or computer science."

"Why not medicine?"

"Well, I like to work with my hands and dentistry is now different from what it used to be. It has advanced tremendously. People used to have their teeth pulled out. Now we preserve them and if any are missing, we use implants."

"Implants", said Jana, "I didn't know that!"

"Well, they have new materials that can make the bone stronger so it can hold the implant. The orthopaedic surgeons inject a bone paste into patients with broken bones, the same thing can be done with the jaw – you can inject the material into the jaw bone to make it stronger, then you can implant one or more teeth. We can also use naturally occuring elements such as stable strontium to strengthen the bone."

"I am not old enough to need that," joked Jana, "my teeth are perfect!"

"If you would like to know, this is one of the things that attracted me to you. It is a pleasure to look at them. As you can see, my teeth are also perfect. I like people with perfect teeth. Of course, this is apart from your personality, which I like even more!"

Jana smiled and looked at him with great affection.

"I really like you, Richard, and I don't know why!"

"I think probably its because I am a nice guy!"

"It must be more than that. Do you believe in astrology?"

" Somewhat."

"When were you born?"

"September 14. Why?"

"Well, you are a Virgo. I was also born in September. People under this sign are usually hard working, persistent, obsessed with detail and like to help others. They help or try

to help without being asked; some people think this is inter-
ference. In reality, I always try to be helpful, but people
misinterpret it."

"Don't worry. I know you by now and I know that you
try your best. Jana, how did you get your name?"

"My parents thought that I might be a boy, and that I
would be called 'Jan' and that I would become some sort of
a leader. Indeed, I became a leader – I was honest and –
people like that. But I was a girl so I became Jana."

"I noticed that you have a very good disposition; you
don't seem to be biased. It is difficult to be unbiased when
you are the leader of a team as a goalie; the girls probably
compete with each other."

"That is true, but I was lucky that I could select my
teammates from the players who applied. Of course, Uta,
who became our coach, was very helpful. I selected them
not only according to their ability to play soccer, but also
depending on their personality, their ability to work with
others. I changed several team members before we left; you
know I can be very critical."

"Oh? Why don't you criticize me?"

"Because you have no faults."

"I have, but you don't see them", he laughed, "you are
in love!"

Jana smiled again and just nodded in agreement.

"I know that you love me, Richard."

"How do you know?"

"I see it in your eyes! When I look at you, I see something glowing – blue stars, she said, looking into his blue eyes.

"I didn't know you were a poet!"

"Only for you, I can write verses, but not for everybody."

"Tell me more about yourself!", Jana pleaded.

"I am an easy-going fellow. I am ambitious, but in a quiet way. I do not like the rat-race."

"Well, maybe we are well suited to one another," suggested Jana.

Actually, she had been thinking about Richard since the day she met him. She came from a small village, not far from Dubrovnik. In her country, many people dream about America and how to get there. Jana always wanted to leave home. She was an enterprising young girl and she saw no limit to her ambition to explore the unknown. She became an engineering student specializing in electronics; but what would she do if she stayed in America, all alone, she asked herself.

"Richard, tell me, what are your plans after the Olympics?"

"Well, you see, I am a Canadian. I will go on studying either at home or at some college nearby."

"You know," said Jana, "I am an engineering student but I have no money to study; the universities are expensive here."

"Yes! But if you are good academically and good in sports, they will take you on a scholarship!"

"Actually, I was very good in soccer, but I would prefer to coach a team. I can better express my potential for leadership."

"Can we get married eventually?" Richard asked.

"We could, but if you are in college, you cannot study and have kids! It is difficult but we don't have to have kids immediately", continued Jana. "One thing that I cannot forget is my teammates. You know, we came here together and I don't want to lose their friendship. We grew up together."

"But you have to look after your own future!"

"I don't know what I will do. How would it be if we promised each other to stay in touch?"

"Yes, but you are beautiful; you will be the centre of attention in the States. You probably will forget me, if you stay here", said Richard.

"Richard! Never! You won my heart after a short acquaintance. We both will study and we'll get together, let's say after a year."

There were many conversations like this and they always ended on the same note: Love without end – they were as good as married because both were dependable, serious people. They knew that they would keep their word.

The next day, Jana was returning with Sumita from soccer practice, and repeated to her the conversation with Richard.

"You know, Sumita, I had a long talk with Richard. He offered to marry me if I stay in America."

Sumita was not surprised.

"Actually, you are always together. You remember the meeting at the Conference Centre? Richard selected you to assist him in finding the plans for Ookk's project. You sort of fit together! But that reminds me, I have to have a talk with Michael. He follows me wherever I go, under any pretext."

That evening, she asked Michael to take a walk with her in the now-famous Wildlife Trails before he took the Olympic bus back to the base. He tried to excuse himself, but she pinned him down because she wanted to have a serious talk. Soccer was her obsession and her future profession, since she was a phys-ed student. She knew that soccer was also Michael's main interest. He told her how he had been declared an MVP and how he had become captain of a soccer team. He had planned to become a soccer coach after he finished playing; however, he had decided to enroll in physical education, which gave him wider opportunities. But he knew that he would always be associated with soccer: teaching soccer, judging soccer, or playing soccer. In Sumita, he found a kindred soul. He knew that she was studying phys-ed – he thought to himself that made a good combination – a man coach for a man's team, and a woman for a women's team – or vice versa.

Sumita was a strong girl, six feet tall, and she had always thought about soccer, not men. But when she met Michael, for her it was like meeting Mr. Soccer himself.

Since he came to visit their camp in Stone Mountain Park, he had always talked about soccer and nothing else. Since she was also into soccer, they talked about her as well. He paid more attention to her than to her friends on the team, who tried to engage him in conversation – the reason being that they also talked about fashion and their looks, while Sumita always talked about soccer.

Sumita was simply enchanted by Michael, by the way he described his games, triumphs, and the defeats. He explained to her the way Americans played and she described to him the European game. What was new to Michael was the way her team played.

"You see, Michael, we had a very good coach at home; a bright fellow who taught us many of the fine points of the game of soccer. We have been lucky to meet him again here in Athens where he was associated with one of the soccer committees. You know him as Kostek, who is training us now."

"The whole team?"

"Yes! Everybody is trained to move forward or go to defence. It is like a wave – that is why it is difficult to stop us."

"I also noticed that you always have three referees on the field!"

"Exactly!" That stops a lot of brutality."

"You must teach me some of your tricks. Maybe I could become a better player."

"Michael! I think you are an excellent player. But there is always room for improvement!"

In endless conversations Michael and Sumita discussed the pros and cons of soccer. But, inadvertently, their thoughts were also directed towards their own future.

"Michael, I was thinking seriously about staying in the U.S.A. but I know relatively little about life here. If I stay, what would be my future?", asked Sumita.

"I told you that if you are bright and a good student, as well as a good sportsman, pardon my expression", Michael laughed, "sports woman, you can get a scholarship at a good university. America needs people like you. Our social system is based on merit. New people come from various countries to Ellis Island in New York and replace those who have already progressed on the social ladder. Obviously, people who emigrate are enterprising. Those who don't succeed, return to their old country without making any progress. I know of others who go home with the money they make here and become the wealthy class in their country."

"I know of such people in my country in Europe. There are many; we call them 'Americans'; they're able to buy their family farm or they start their own business", interjected Sumita.

"You are so right," continued Michael, "However most people prefer to stay here. That is the luck of North America: a natural selection of enterprising individuals who wish to succeed. They have to work hard and to make sacrifices, but if they are willing, the majority do well. It certainly isn't easy though!"

"Do you think this system of immigrant influx will continue?"

"I am sure it will, unless our society degenerates into drugs, alcoholism, or greed or the other deadly sins."

"Michael, my family is Greek- Orthodox. This is a result of the Turkish occupation of our country; my ancestors were Greeks who opposed the Turks. Would that pose a problem for me?" Sumita asked.

"Frankly, I don't think so", answered Michael. "We have people of all sorts of nationalities and religions. The U.S.A. is indeed a melting pot. Most recent immigrants are Asians, Chinese or Vietnamese; they work hard and I am sure this will be the current cultural group that will succeed."

"I understand what you mean," concluded Sumita. "But how is daily life here? I noticed that almost everybody is in a rush, an endless rush, with no time for relaxation."

"You're right, but this is the U.S. culture. In Canada, life is slower, but the economic opportunities are less attractive. Actually, one of the current problems in the U.S. is what to do with people who cannot work because they are too old, too sick, or simply don't want to work."

"What is the Government doing to do with these people?", asked Sumita.

"I don't know. Entertain them, I guess, provide some sort of occupational therapy. Our entertainment industry is enormous. I am glad, because I myself like to watch television. The difficulty with 'watching' T.V. or pursuing other non-productive and passive activities is that it may erode the enterprising spirit of America. If we become a 'watcher' society rather than a 'doer' society, other countries will do the work and will bypass us."

"Michael," said Sumita interrupting him, "we are supposed to talk about our personal matters, but you are instead giving me a lecture on the social history of the United States. Anyhow, I am sure that I would like to stay in the States, if I could live with you. However, we do not know our future; and maybe it is better not to know!"

"You're talking like you are expecting a soccer injury! Don't be pessimistic. Eventually, everything turns out alright. Can you promise me that if you decide to live in U.S., you will consider me as your partner?"

Sumita looked at him with great affection. "I assure you, Mike, that I will."

***

CHAPTER 14

ONCE the decision was made that Ookk should proceed without Uta's help in his efforts to build the "Monument to all Mothers", as it was called now, he became more audacious in his efforts. He actually was not alone. Everybody in the camp, whenever he met them, inquired if any progress had been made. No one knew about his recent conversation with Uta, except Jana, Sumita and Kostek. However, as happens in any small community which is sort of isolated, the cooling of the relations between Ookk and Uta was noticed. Before their "long talk", they were together almost all the time, they discussed things before they let others know what they were going to do; they also made all trips together, be it in Stone Mountain Park, the Olympic Village, or to Athens.

The Prutenian team members considered Ookk as sort of an escort to Uta. They were not jealous of her, but did not fully comprehend why they suddenly were spending much less time together. Everyone sensed that their relationship had changed but no one suggested or discussed why. In their fervour to practice soccer, they seemed to forget that since Uta had to be at the soccer field, she could not be with Ookk. What they did not understand was why Ookk seemed suddenly to lose interest in soccer and did not attend their soccer practices. In reality, Ookk spent a lot of time at the camp, talking most of the time to Abercorn, who was almost constantly present, arranging "things" for the girls, and talking to visitors who were coming in greater numbers to see Ookk. For Abercorn, Ookk was a hero; the subject of his admiration was mostly Ookk's plane. He became an expert in explaining to visitors how the plane operated and gladly posed for photographs with the aircraft. He couldn't tell them much about Mars, except that the giant Martians were simply brutes and that we should be happy not to have them on Earth, and that Ookk was happy to "escape" from Mars.

Ookk was also a hero for many other people in Atlanta. The fact that he appeared in some photographs with African-Americans increased his popularity in the city. "This man likes everybody" people said. It was mostly the curiosity value of someone who claimed that he's from another planet.

Ookk was actually not wasting any time. In his usual methodical way, he was gathering information about Atlanta, its resources, its organizations, and its important people. If 'Tara', in the movie 'Gone with the Wind' of which he had heard about in Atlanta was the inspiration for the Antebellum Plantation at Stone Mountain Park, perhaps his arrival could initiate the Mara building. He liked more and more, the new name for his project conceived during the meeting at the Evergreen Convention Centre.

In the course of the next few days, he made numerous calls to the people at the Atlanta Chamber of Commerce, the Mayor's office and the Olympic Committee; they provided him with a wealth of information. He found them extremely cooperative. They were all thinking about the period after the end of the Olympics. Bill Campbell, the energetic mayor of Atlanta actually sent him several notes. Abercorn gladly served as a messenger to the City Hall, telling everybody there what a fantastic person Ookk was. Actually, Ookk found the relationship between the black and white people in Atlanta quite peaceful. Nothing resembling the Los Angeles riots! In a sense, these were "two solitudes" but both parties understood that it was to their mutual advantage to promote Atlanta's economy, for which peace was necessary.

Ookk was actually planning how to present his project to the public while the Olympics were taking place. He thought more and more of taking his plane to the newly-created Olympic Park in downtown Atlanta, next to the Atlanta Convention Complex. He understood that such a step must be carefully thought out and executed. "For instance", he wondered, "what will I show the people if they ask me about the project?". Tolek, the virtual reality man, told him that creating an IMAX screen at the Olympic Park on short notice was impractical. "Even if I show them the picture of the model, people will like to have a memento of their visit."

Then a brilliant idea flashed in his mind. How about giving them a souvenir of his visit to Earth? He remembered that when he had visited the Olympic Village, an active exchange of all sorts of souvenirs was one of the major activities among the visitors. He also remembered that Nancy Nolan, when she came to the Stone Mountain Convention Centre, brought with her Jay Greenspoon, a manufacturer of souvenirs. "What can I lose, if I were to talk to the man and suggest to him that I could sell his souvenirs at the Olympic Park." Naturally, it would be Ookk's idea to help to promote his project. He thought of a round medal of reddish colour, since Mars is round and has a reddish hue. The inscription around the rim would read MONUMENT TO ALL MOTHERS, WITH LOVE FROM PLANET MARS.

"Nine words," he thought. The size of the medal would be determined by the number of words around the perimeter.

Ookk was not a man to wait once he decided on something. When Michael came to the camp the next morning, he asked him whether he would like to fly with him to Atlanta. Naturally, he told everybody at breakfast about his plans; all the team members thought the idea was excellent. They looked at Jana and asked whether they could go to Atlanta to "watch' Ookk's plane, but Kostek answered instead.

"You better come with me to soccer practice. There are only a few days left. There is no question of any absenteeism. You cannot be taken off the team since there are no replacements. The only replacement for one of you would be Uta and that's only if one of you sustains a fracture. You have to learn to play 'faultless' in order not to get a yellow ticket. Richard will go with us since he has been the referee at our practice and Michael can go with Ookk to Atlanta."

Uta approved of this plan. In reality, she had no choice but to approve it since she was not involved in the decision. Actually, she was on the verge of crying but she did not show her emotions. "That's perfect", she said applauding Ookk ostentatiously.

Right after breakfast, Ookk took the plane out of the bushes, readied it for flight, and took off, as always, straight into the sky.

It was exciting to observe Atlanta from the air during the Olympic Games. The streets were full of pedestrians, sightseeing and shopping; numerous souvenir and novelty stores dotted the corners. The highways were full of cars, and some streets were obviously closed to car traffic. They could see the runners competing at the Olympic Stadium, which was filled to capacity. Every seat, as expected, was occupied. While flying over the stadium, they observed an accident. A man taking part in the vault jumping suddenly fell to the ground and remained motionless; this occurred in the far left corner of the Stadium field, away from the runners who, on that day, were participating in the 100-meter run, the same event which made Jesse Owens famous in Berlin some sixty years before.

Ookk made a momentous decision. Knowing that he needed only about a twenty-foot-square space for landing, he descended on a spot next to the accident, in full view of the hundreds of thousand of spectators. It was a bold move but, since he arrived before they even had called the ambulance at the other end of the Stadium, most people, including the officials, thought that this was a planned rescue operation. Ookk and Michael quickly jumped out of the

195

plane and approached the accident victim on the ground, who happened to be from Kenya. The man had sustained a serious injury to his chest from the vaulting pole, but the reason for his motionlessness was a possibly broken right hip. Michael, who had taken a first aid course, knew that in such cases it was important to move the patient as little as possible, because if it was a fracture, an artery could be injured and he could begin to bleed on the spot. Fortunately, Ookk was very ingenious and was quick to respond to crisis situations. He had a large blanket in his plane, on which the injured athlete was placed. In the meantime, a young doctor from the Olympic Medical Service arrived on the scene. He fully approved of the action taken. He had with him a syringe with an analgesic, which he injected into the injured athlete.

"Which hospital should I take him to?", Ookk asked, with a look of tremendous competence on his face, as if carrying out a routine task.

"Piedmont Hospital," came back the reply. The young doctor appeared somewhat flabbergasted by the appearance of Ookk's aircraft.

"Would you like to come with us?", Ookk asked.

"I would like to come, but since you have a paramedic," he answered, pointing to Michael, "I will supervise the loading of the patient and the emergency doctors will supervise the unloading at arrival in the hospital."

"By the way, Piedmont Hospital has a helicopter landing pad on the roof", he added.

"Thank you, but I do not need one" answered Ookk. "We go straight to Emergency."

Ookk did not want to argue about the landing site. The athlete's pain had already subsided due to the injection of morphine. He was carefully moved unto the blanket and was carried in a horizontal position by eight people and then placed in the aircraft. With Michael sitting next to him, the plane took off again in full view of all the spectators. Some people, who were watching the 100-meter run events, did not even notice the commotion related to the accident, and the Olympic competitions continued. Abercorn, who was left behind, just walked with the doctor to the Medical Service Station. The doctor, a young surgeon from the same Piedmont Hospital, asked Abercorn about Ookk and his plane, and about who had "arranged" this service; he did not say "authorize" and Abercorn tried to remain as taciturn as possible. There were no reporters at the Medical Service Station. Abercorn spent the rest of the day there at the invitation of the doctor and enjoyed observing the events from an excellent position. However, when he was returning to Stone Mountain Park that evening, he picked up some newspapers which already had pictures of the landing of Ookk's plane. There were also articles about a "Dramatic Rescue of an Injured Athlete by the Martian Pilot" and about "Martian Strikes Again: Always Ready to Help."

In the meantime, Ookk landed the plane on the lawn in front of the Emergency Department of Piedmont Hospital. The commotion was unbelievable.

The orthopaedic surgeon on duty was right on the spot. He immediately ordered X-rays and the diagnosis was confirmed.

He came back to talk to the athlete who was still slightly groggy after the injection, but was able to answer all the questions.

"Before you operate, you will have to call my team leader." the athlete requested. This was done and then the surgeon explained the diagnosis to him and the patient.

"We have to do hip pinning." He explained in detail what the operation involved and showed them the X-ray where a fracture of the neck of the hip bone was evident. He praised Ookk for bringing the patient immediately to the hospital.

"You see, in any accident or heart attack, time is of the essence. The patient could die while waiting for transport. It is very difficult for ambulances to get through city traffic. In the country, it is even more difficult to get immediate help", commented the surgeon.

"But you do have helicopter ambulances", said Michael.

"Yes, but you have to call them at the airport; then they have to go to the site of the accident and fly to the hospital. This is very time consuming."

"In Vienna they post ambulances all across the city in strategic locations, so that they can take patients from specific districts to the hospital. We do not have this system here," continued the doctor.

Ookk explained to him that his air-plane used ordinary gasoline.

"This is why I don't have to go to the airport. Wherever I am, I can go directly to the hospital."

The conversation then turned to the method of operation which was going to be used in surgery.

"You mean you will pin the two pieces of bone together?" Ookk asked.

"Yes, but in addition, we are happy to use a new method", answered the doctor. This is a type of bone paste."

"Bone paste?"

"Yes, you see, it is called the Norian Skeletal Repair System. The material used is called Dahlite, which is similar in composition to natural bone minerals. One can inject the site of a fracture and it will temporarily unite the broken bone fragments."

"Temporarily? But don't we need a permanent union?"

"Yes," explained the doctor, "but the bone paste, though similar to natural bone, is still a foreign material. Anything foreign is either rejected or absorbed by the body. The advantage of Dahlite is that when it is absorbed, the bone cells build normal bone at the same location. This temporary union is very useful; it helps heal the fracture. The bone paste can be placed in areas of acute fracture, such as in this case, and it is reinforced by putting in a pin that unites the fracture."

"Then why bother putting a pin?"

"This is a precaution; the material is new. At this moment, its usefulness is to help heal fractures."

The surgeon then left to see the patient in the operating room while Ookk and Michael waited with friends of the injured athlete.

"It's a terrible accident", commented Ookk. "To come so far, from Africa, and not to be able to participate in the games is a sad situation."

"Well," answered Michael, "accidents can happen and do happen anywhere. There are worse diseases, however, such as cancer or diabetes, or arteriosclerosis."

When the doctor returned with the news that the operation had gone well, he turned his attention to Ookk:

"It was very good that you brought the patient immediately to the hospital with your plane. The sooner they are treated, the better. Time is of the essence. I understand that you are originally from Mars? How do you treat this type of injury on Mars?"

Ookk became very taciturn. "We don't", he answered. "I am one of the Macrocells; we are products of cell culture. If one of us gets injured, we are disposed of by being placed on the Martian surface and left to die."

That sounded terrible to all concerned, but they did not comment and the surgeon did not ask Ookk any further questions. To change the subject, Michael asked the surgeon some questions of interest to him.

"Tell me, doctor, twenty years ago, when a person was sixty-five, that was considered old. Now, you have to be eighty to be classified as "old". Scientists have worked on old-age diseases quite a lot, I guess, so there is constant progress?"

"Yes," answered the doctor, "I happen to also work in research. One thing that, hopefully, will be conquered is hardening of the arteries; if it occurs in the brain, it is called Alzheimer's. We are already making progress, but before we treat a disease, we have to understand the underlying mechanisms; this is called basic research, now carried on a submolecular level."

"It is good to be here, much better than to be on Mars", answered Michael. "Even the astronauts, if they get sick, have to come down to Earth for treatment. If I may ask, can you tell me what is cancer?"

"Well, cancer is a degenerative disease of old age; it occurs very rarely in young people", answered the doctor. "The current interest is in genetic damage as a factor in the causation of cancer. Genetics are important, but personally, I think that this is only one of the factors involved. The problem is so complex that I don't think that anyone understands it completely."

"But my medical friend, Maria, tells me that we don't know everything about diabetes, but we can still treat it?"

"Yes", the doctor answered. "Diabetes is a different condition: it is a deficiency of the hormone that controls blood sugar level. A Canadian scientist, Frederick Banting found that by injecting extracts which contain this hormone, insulin, you can correct the deficiency."

Those who were listening, including the Kenyans, were very interested in the comments made by the doctor.

"I know one thing: exercise and diet helps everybody live longer", said the Kenyan coach, with whom Ookk had become friendly. "Why don't you come to Kenya?" he asked Ookk. "We have gliders with wings, but nothing like your aircraft. Our country is very mountainous; this type of aircraft would be very useful."

"I think the first use on Earth of my 'Sursum' would be in the manner that we used it today, as an ambulance," said Ookk. "This was the first air rescue flight on Earth with this type of plane."

Ookk did promise to visit him at some future time. But, by now, he had so many invitations that he did not know when he would be able to go to Africa. The list of people extending invitations to him was growing rapidly.

At this point, they parted company. When Ookk returned to Stone Mountain Camp, everybody had heard about his "air rescue mission". Abercorn showed them the newspapers describing the event:

"Heroic Air Rescue Mission on an Injured Athlete."

"Ookk Does it Again, Helping People."

Ookk was very proud that he had accomplished the mission without any help from Uta. He did it all on his own and did not hide his pride.

***

CHAPTER 15

SINCE Ookk's plan to contact Jay Greenspoon the day before was put off by the rescue mission, he phoned him the following morning to discuss the production of Martian souvenirs.

"Hi, Jay", he said. "This is Ookk. Do you remember me from the meeting at Stone Mountain Park? I would like discuss my project for the 'Monument to All Mothers' with you."

"Any time, Ookk!' Of course, I not only remember you, but now you are a famous man. Yesterday, I read an article about you in the Atlanta Journal, about how you rescued an injured athlete and flew him directly from the Olympic Stadium to the Piedmont Hospital. Come over and we can have a chat. But tell me one thing: why didn't you tell everybody at the meeting that you are a Martian?"

"Actually, there are two reasons: one is that I am not one of the Giant Martians but a product of cell culture on

Mars. Secondly, I thought that if I claimed to be a Martian, you would not take my project seriously", answered Ookk.

"Well, I must admit that I would have been surprised to hear that; the people from the Atlanta Chamber of Commerce would be even more surprised. They would have thought it was a joke. Now, it's a different situation. Your origin is common knowledge; whether people believe it or not is of secondary importance; the fact is that the project you are proposing is good and it will be good for Atlanta after the Olympics are finished. But what can I do to help you?"

"I will tell you when I see you. Uta is now immersed one hundred percent in soccer practice with Kostek. I don't think I will take my plane. Could you meet me and Michael at the Georgia Tech MARTA Station? That is the only place I know with certainty. I will bring Mike or Richard with me for company, if they are free."

"OK, I will see you in two hours, allowing for travel time from Stone Mountain. I will be driving my great Saturn", answered Jay.

Ookk and Michael took the bus from Stone Mountain Park to the MARTA terminal station and arrived at Georgia Tech sooner than they expected. While they were waiting for Jay to arrive, several people approached Ookk for his autograph. He gladly obliged, but since he always carried his book to register supporters for his project, he also collected more signatures in return. Jay drove them to his souvenir-pin factory. Outside it was an inconspicuous building, but inside it was pleasantly arranged and immaculately clean.

Yes! I want to join the 1996 Olympic Games Pin Society.

Name   John OOKK

Address Youth Camping Grounds

City STONE MOUNTAIN PARK   State GEORGIA

Zip Code   30086

Phone = (   )   Nil

[X] I'm enclosing my check for $19.96* made out to the 1996 Olympic Games Pin Society.

[ ] Please bill my VISA¹ card for $19.96.
My account number is: _____
The expiration date is: _____
Authorized signature: _____

Or call 1-800-PINS-4-96 (800-746-7496). Have your VISA® card ready.

THE 1996 OLYMPIC GAMES PIN SOCIETY IS AN OFFICIAL LICENSED PRODUCT OF THE ATLANTA COMMITTEE FOR THE OLYMPIC GAMES AND IS MADE POSSIBLE THROUGH THE SUPPORT OF THE COCA-COLA COMPANY.

Satisfaction Guaranteed. You'll begin receiving your membership benefits within eight weeks. Void where prohibited or limited by law. If you wish to cancel your membership you may do so within 7 days. ©1994 The Coca-Cola Company. *U.S. dollars only, please do not send cash. Includes applicable shipping and sales tax.

Mail this form, or
Call 1-800-PINS-4-96

Jay showed them his shop. The production of souvenir pins took place in a large hall, where a conveyor belt with a stamping machine produced the pins. Several women sat around the belt, carrying out various functions: inspecting for quality, placing the colours, attaching the holding pin, sorting and packaging. It was obviously a very well-organized operation.

Ookk was very impressed. It was the first time that he had seen a manufacturing process.

"You are almost completely automated", Ookk commented. "However, you do have personal inspection for quality control which is very important? I like the decorations on the wall and the fact that you play soft background music. It is very relaxing."

Jay was happy with his comments. "I had to make quite a few improvements in the operation before I reached this stage. We have to compete with foreign manufacturers, so my operation must be very efficient. I also want to tell you that the employees can choose what music they want to hear; they decide by majority vote, so everything's very democratic and it makes for a pleasant working atmosphere. What you see on the walls are designs of different pins which I make or have bought."

"You are an inventive man, Jay", commented Michael who, so far had refrained from making any comments. "I am sure you can make further improvements to make colour printing easier. There is always room for improvement, for nothing is perfect. What I like about your pins is that they convey a message. Personally, I prefer pins that are easily deciphered and not crowded with details that cannot be recognized by an onlooker. For instance, here you have a pin inscribed 'Canada', showing a mounted policeman. Richard told me that the Royal Canadian Mounted Police is a symbol of Canada and it is unique to that country. Another pin I like in your collection is a pin showing a bird with the inscription 'Bermuda' this indicates that one usually flies to Bermuda, although you can also get there by boat~, The pin with the inscription 'Ski Vermont', showing a skier, actually does not need the word 'Ski' because you are portraying a skier."

Jay laughed. After they went to his office and sat down for a cup of coffee, the conversation continued: "Your comments are excellent, Mike you must be quite an expert on souvenir pins. Now, I would like to hear about Ookk's impressions of life in the United States. To be truthful, I am not interested in Mars. I think we have other priorities on Earth. I am unlikely to go to Mars, even if people live there!"

"I am surprised," answered Ookk. "Most people I talk to want to know how life goes on Mars. They seem to think that it might be better than on Earth; they seem to be dissatisfied with their own life. I always tell them that my life was very boring and that I find life on Earth much more interesting!"

"I understand that," continued Jay. "The extra-terrestrial expeditions they watch on T.V. make them believe that they could go to a 'better planet' and live there, which I think is nonsense. We have many problems here, as you know, but these are not serious enough to warrant leaving Earth. People generally are not satisfied with their lives. The grass, as they say is always greener on the other side. In the U.S, people move around a lot, looking for a better place to live. But, maybe we should return to the subject of your visit, Ookk. What can I do for you? I can guess that, since you came here, you want pins to promote your project. Is that correct?"

"Yes," answered Ookk. "I think having a symbolic pin would be a good idea, but I want to have your opinion as to what sort of pin it should be."

"There are two ways of looking at it. You could either make a pin showing a model of your building in the form of a human body, or you could make a pin reminding people that you are from Mars," answered Jay.

"How would it be if we combined the two ideas?", Ookk asked. "The pin could be round because Mars is round, probably reddish in colour because Mars is seen as a star with a reddish hue. Around the rim, an inscription could be placed reading:

"A MEMENTO OF MEETING OOKK FROM PLANET MARS: MONUMENT TO ALL MOTHERS."

"If it's not too expensive, you could also have a picture of the model of the proposed building."

"Your suggestions are excellent," answered Jay. "I know that you don't have any money, so I would charge you only for the cost of production. I can eventually recover the costs if you sell enough pins."

"I was planning to sell them to donate money for the building", interjected Ookk.

"Don't worry about it; you can deduct your expenses for the production of the pins. I don't wish to make any money on you; I just want to contribute to your project."

"By the way," Mike asked, "what is the name of your company?"

"SOUVENIR FOREVER".

"Very good name, Jay," said Mike. "People are wearing more and more pins; it used to be buttons, now it's pins. I am sure your business will be booming. Even Martian pins will be good advertising for you. Ookk is very grateful for your help. It is for a good cause. I am sure my mother will be happy to hear that a monument will be built for all mothers, including my mother and Richard's mother."

"You know, Ookk", Jay continued the conversation, "I have big plans for my factory. I am alone; my wife died of cancer, the children are grown up. My life revolves around making souvenir pins. There are all sorts of pins which, I think, may be in demand and nobody is making them. They could also be worn as costume jewellery without any inscription, such as a flower of a State, which in Georgia would undoubtedly be the Cherokee Rose. We do have pins of various countries: the U.S.A., Japan, Germany, France, Canada. We have sports pins, but relatively few commemorating events, such as the Indianapolis Car Race, or the St. Lawrence River Seadoo Racing; we could also make city pins or convocation pins."

"I agree with that," answered Ookk. "I am sure you saw the people trading pins. They like to show off the places they have been to. Some wore hats full of pins and they have everybody looking at them."

211

"Ookk, I would like to hire you as my Public Relations man", said Jay. "You are now well known in Atlanta and since you are tall, one cannot help but notice your presence. A Mars pin worn by anyone becomes a topic of conversation and that is all that matters. I cannot do everything myself. Actually, I was thinking of employing some of the girls from Prutenia, because they speak several languages, and because we have such a multilingual society in the U.S.. But we have such strict immigration laws which do not recognize the needs of all businesses."

"We have to protect the jobs of Americans," answered Mike. "I am sure that many of the athletes who are here would like to stay in the U.S.A., if they were permitted."

"On Mars," interjected Ookk, "we can't even move from one place to another. If you want to change your job, that is physically impossible because everybody is trained in a certain skill. We have to work for our living, more or less."

"Unfortunately, since some people prefer not to work at all, we have so many that are constantly unemployed. You know, Jay, if you want, Richard and I can talk to the girls and ask them if they would like to stay here." (Mike at this point was thinking primarily of Sumita and Jana). "They all seem to be so impressed with the American way of life!"

"It would be very difficult," answered Jay. "I could not employ them in the factory. My workers are quite good and I would not want them to lose their jobs, even if your friends worked more efficiently."

"But you stated that you would like to expand your operation", Michael continued the discussion. "The Prutenian girls have various professions, like engineering, architecture, music, and medicine; they would work on a different level than your team. Perhaps, to follow your idea, they could design pins for various professions, since they know what the people who are engaged in these professions want. For instance, Maria is a medical student; I am sure she could come up with designs for pins which would appeal to neurologists, cardiologists, or surgeons. Sumita, my girl-friend, is in physical education. I have not seen any pins promoting for example cricket or seadooing specifically. I think it would be like hiring twelve consultants at a very good price."

Jay was taken aback by Michael's comments. He liked the idea of expanding his operation, but he did not understand exactly what function Michael had in mind for his prospective employees.

"Do you mean that they would not work here physically, but rather submit their designs or proposals, and if they are accepted, I would pay them? Well, this may be possible; it is completely different from what I thought you would ask me. But you have to realize that they would have to have sufficient money for their room and board, more or less. I don't think they would have any other major expenses. It is important that they not be on the public purse", concluded Jay.

"Exactly", answered Michael. "I know all that and I would not want you to go to any trouble. I think such an arrangement would be good for your company and good for the Prutenian girls. I have known them for several weeks. If you can trust my judgment, I have never met a more enterprising and congenial bunch. I think it would be worthwhile to try to keep them here."

Jay was not completely convinced, being a careful businessman. He knew of Michael's attachment to Sumita so he understood the arguments which Michael brought up.

"Let's not rush into anything", Jay continued. "Most things work themselves out, as the Scots say. We have to plan carefully how to approach the authorities, and the plan has to be very sensible. If you ask me, I would say that Ookk's presence would help them more than anything else. How can you propose something like this, Michael, without talking to the girls first? Maybe they don't really want to stay here."

"From what Uta told me, most athletes attending the Olympics would like to stay here", interjected Ookk. "All that Michael is saying is that you will not find more loyal employees, and loyalty is one of the most important factors in any undertaking."

Jay did not comment at this point, but started to think seriously about his proposal. Since he had met Ookk at the meeting at Stone Mountain Park, he somehow felt that this man would change his life. "Perhaps it was a premonition or some Martian influence", he thought. "Ookk came here to see me about making a Martian pin. I am sure that this was not just a pretext to come here, because we have agreed on what sort of souvenir pin he will need. Now, they bring up the question of the Prutenian team working for him."

Jay then drove Ookk and Michael in his big car to the Georgia Tech MARTA station. They boarded the MARTA

214

train through Atlanta, all the way to the terminus, and then took the bus to the Stone Mountain camp. On the way, they had a chance to discus the proposal that entered the conversation unexpectedly.

"What do you think about the whole thing, Ookk?", Michael asked.

"Well, I think that maybe we will be able to convince Jay. Perhaps you were too aggressive, the way you spoke to him. He is an elderly man, living alone and satisfied with his situation. He does not need any more money. Why should he get himself into a new venture?"

"You have not grasped what drives Americans, Ookk," replied Michael. "It is not only the money. It is the ambition to do more. Look at the people in Atlanta! They seem to derive satisfaction from accomplishing certain tasks and, if possible, to accomplish them promptly."

"I play soccer, which I hope will be my profession. Of course, I would like to get more money, but I do it mainly because I like to do well whatever I do. Jay has the ambition to do more because he would derive some satisfaction if the new pins would be better than those made by other people."

"Maybe you are right, Michael. But Jay is right when he said that probably my presence would help them more than anyone else. Don't forget that people look at me as a curiosity, and that curiosity has great commercial value."

"You're right, Ookk. You don't have to worry about yourself. You can probably travel around the world free of charge. Even the Chinese or the Russians would welcome you. You've already been invited to Kenya. But, apart from that, you have friends. Richard and I will never forget you.

You know what a Roman philosopher once said? 'When fortune is fickle, faithful friends are found'. And we are your friends."

***

CHAPTER 16

OOKK did not want to postpone any longer his plan to proceed with the preparation for building the "Monument to All Mothers", as it was called. His discussion with Jay Greenspoon encouraged him greatly.

Ookk convinced himself that he could act independently of Uta. For him, this was a great psychological victory. Gone was his inferiority complex and his timidity. He methodically prepared his plan to promote the project, with the help of the ever ingenious Abercorn. Abercorn printed thousands of postcards for him, showing a picture of the model of the proposed building. The pictures looked very impressive. He also obtained, with Abercorn's help, many simple sheet-albums for collecting signatures and addresses of people who were willing to endorse his project.

However, Ookk also knew that the general public was unaware of the value of education; most people want to learn in order to get a better job, but they do not appreciate the intrinsic value of knowledge. He realized that telling people not to get or take drugs would have little effect and would be mostly ignored. With two million attending the Olympics, he also remembered that most of the people he would be meeting would not be from Atlanta, but from all over the world. How could he explain to the visitors that his interactive education in Atlanta would eventually expand to their countries and, therefore that his project would help them indirectly by conveying the message how to avoid common human vices? He was thinking of CNN News, which is headquartered in Atlanta, and what a powerful message can be delivered from here to 150 countries. He could see himself giving a speech in front of the "Monument for All Mothers", which would be transmitted all over the world.

Ookk decided to wear his Martian space uniform for the Olympic Park presentation, since it was different from anything seen on Earth. Novelty seeking is so common, that the more he impressed visitors, he thought, the more likely they were to support his project. He also felt that the Martian medals, as he called them, were an excellent idea from the viewpoint of promotion. To get a person's attention, a souvenir pin would be more effective than any pictures or speeches. "The medium is the message", he thought quoting Marshall McLuhan; the medium in this case would be the souvenir pin, it would be something to take home, a memento of their visit.

Ookk wondered whether he should collect any money. He found out from Michael that anything with a value of less than one dollar was not taxable; it became obvious to him that the price should be ninety-nine cents. The figure of "ninety-nine cents" stuck in his mind because he had seen this amount so frequently in shop windows. In any case, since he was turning over almost all the money to the City of Atlanta, except for a refund of expenses, there should be no conflict of interest, nor could he be accused of trying to get rich. The sole purpose of the project was to acquaint the public, particularly the leaders of the Atlanta community, with the world problems to be presented in the exhibits.

The final question was who should assist him at the Olympic Park. Obviously, he needed some help. He had lost the close contact he had with the Prutenian team; he saw them the morning before they went to soccer practice and then at night, when the discussion centred mostly on soccer. However, he did have a chance to talk things over with Kostek. During the day, Ookk usually went to the Evergreen Convention Centre to talk with Mr. Ericsson, whom he liked more and more on closer acquaintance. His other favourite spot was the athletic grounds, where he chatted with the visitors. Many people knew him from the articles they had read in the local newspapers. However, there were many foreigners who met him for the first time, because they did not read English. He also listened to the T.V. News, which gave a good summary of the daily events. These encounters helped him to gain confidence by being aware what was going on. However, if he wanted the help of Uta and her team, he would have to re-establish his contact with them. Uta, at this time, was totally influenced by Kostek, who was training the team intensively in preparation for the exhibition game. It became obvious to him that he would have to take this matter up with the Polish soccer coach. One evening, he approached him.

"Kostek," he said, "the girls are practicing soccer every day. Why don't you give them a break?"

"I can't," answered Kostek, "but I do know from Michael about your conversation with Jay. News travels fast in a small community! Since the girls probably do want to stay in the U.S., steps should be taken to make sure they get better exposure to the public. Your presentations at the Olympic Park would be helpful in this respect. I have already spoken to Uta and we agreed that they should go with you to the Park to help you out. By the way, I am sure that Uta is dying to show you her affection", he added jokingly.

Next morning, Ookk donned his Martian space uniform, took Uta and Michael with him and flew to the Olympic Park. Since the Park was surrounded by skyscrapers – the nearby CNN Complex and the Convention Centre – the landing was difficult, but he managed to get down close to the entrance of the twenty-three-acre, newly constructed facility. As soon as the aircraft came to a stop, a crowd of visitors surrounded them. They timed their landing so that the Prutenian team, with Kostek and Richard, were already waiting for them.

After deplaning, Ookk gave a short speech to the assembled crowd, which he actually repeated every 20 or 30 minutes.

"Ladies and Gentlemen," he said. "We want to build a 'Monument to All Mothers' in Atlanta. All of you have mothers. The exhibits to be constructed in the building will help mothers to deal with their problems, mostly created by their children, regardless of their age; they will show the human problems to which they are exposed and how to deal with them."

"Here, you can see the picture of the building. You can obtain it, complete with an autograph for ninety-nine cents. If you want to spend another ninety-nine cents, you can get a commemorative Martian medal. If you support this idea, please sign this book with your address."

Usually, there was general applause. There was no point giving long speeches, because many of the onlookers were from foreign countries: Spanish, French, German, Italian, Japanese, and other nationalities. It soon became apparent that most people wanted to get a souvenir rather than a picture. Some of them tried to bargain for the souvenir pin in exchange for their own pin, but the attempts were not accepted by the Prutenian girls, who circulated in the crowd, collecting signatures. However, many people, mainly from Atlanta, also bought the postcards with the picture of the model, which Ookk was busy autographing. The place was a hubbub of activity, much like a marketplace. People asked Ookk where he came from, to which he simply replied:

"From Mars – as it is written on the Martian Medal." Some people laughed, others spoke to the girls asking when they would be playing their soccer game. There was a mood of jubilation and joviality and no serious questions were asked about Ookk's Martian origin. Everyone admired his space uniform. Local people thought that his performance was a part of the Olympic entertainment program. The demand for "Martian medals" was so great that Ookk had to send one of the girls with a message to Jay to make more of them; it was obvious that demand would exceed the supply.

It was interesting to observe the Prutenian girls as they collected the signatures. Most people did not want to sign anything, but gladly printed their name and address. Some of the strangers had cards with their names and addresses, obviously used for such occasions; this greatly facilitated the spelling of foreign names. Hundreds of names were collected before the evening was over and Ookk then departed from the stadium with Uta and Michael. The girls, with Kostek and Richard, stayed behind and continued the conversations, telling people that Ookk would be back tomorrow and that they should come back if they wanted his autograph. Naturally, the evening papers reported the events.

Next morning, Ookk repeated his performance. He was actually better in talking with foreigners than to locals. The Prutenian girls were of great help, because they spoke several foreign languages, including Italian, Greek and German, and of course the southern slavonic languages. Kostek spoke Polish, Slovak, Czech and Russian. Many of the visitors from Japan, the Far East, and Africa, spoke broken English; everything was acceptable these days, including gesticulation and "sign" language, which led to quite a few jokes and misunderstandings.

Once again, every half-hour or so, Ookk repeated his speech, but hardly anyone listened. The main public relation activities were autographing the picture of the model, distributing the "Martian medals" and, of course, collecting names and addresses of people in attendance.

The story of Ookk's collecting signatures of people who supported the idea of a "Monument to All Mothers" was now known to almost everybody in Atlanta. In the general confusion, the identity of who sponsored the event was lost; some people thought it was the Atlanta Olympic Committee, others thought it was the Chamber of Commerce, or the International Olympic Committee. Ookk's initiative never came up. The general opinion was that there was somebody important behind this; it was too big an undertaking.

Early in the afternoon, Bill Campbell, the Mayor of Atlanta, came to the site. To his surprise, before he had a chance to ask Ookk about his project, he handed him three thousand dollars, which had been collected from the people of Atlanta as a symbolic donation to the 'Monument to All Mothers'.

The Mayor was overcome by the spontaneous enthusiasm of the event. He gave a short speech, thanking Ookk.

"Any contribution to the City is greatly welcome", he said. "You will understand that I cannot underwrite just any project on behalf of the City. However, your initiative to help Atlanta in the after birth activity as I refer to post-Olympic period is greatly appreciated."

With these words, Bill Campbell and several officials accompanying him, signed Ookk's "guest book", as he called it, and were presented with the "Martian medals" and pictures of the model.

Ookk had the opportunity to meet several other prominent Atlantans who are known not only in the United States but also internationally. He was delighted to meet world renowned figures such as the President of Federation international de Football. Dr. Havelonge told Ookk:

"I have heard about you on NBC news", he said. "I don't believe you are from Mars, but your idea to create a 'Monument to All Mothers' in Atlanta, with interactive exhibits, is good."

"It is your prerogative not to believe in my origin", Ookk answered. "In any case, the fact that you think my idea is good, means a great deal to me."

Ookk decided to continue his presentation for the next three days, during which thousands of names and addresses were collected. Curiously, but perhaps understandably, no one seemed to be against his idea. First of all, the building was to be constructed after the Olympics, which occupied everyone's mind at the moment. Secondly, who could oppose the idea of a "Monument to All Mothers"? Anybody who objected would be despised by his own mother, grandmother or mother-in-law. It is known that women were in the majority and their voices are certainly well heard.

The other visitor, whom Ookk was happy to see, was President Samaranch. By now, he knew everything about Ookk's success in Atlanta.

"I told you when we met at the Hilton Hotel, that you would do well and you have. You have certainly contributed to the promotion of the Centennial Games. You are now known internationally and everybody is wondering where you are from", he added jokingly.

He graciously accepted the "Martian medal" and promised Ookk that he would give his idea for "post-Olympic" development a great deal of thought.

"Whether your project will go ahead, I do not know, but your proposals certainly make sense: to engage sports in combatting human vices."

The subject of sports as an antidote to human problems has received wide attention in the media, and the idea has already been planted in many minds. Some members of the International Olympic Committee said that they would expand on the idea.

"These are men of vision", thought Ookk.

***

CHAPTER 17

THE fact that Ookk became known to everybody in Atlanta worked against him in an episode which occurred after the completion of his presentation at the Olympic Park.

On this memorable evening, he was returning alone from Atlanta, because Michael had to stay there. He usually never travelled alone but, obviously, it had to happen on this day.

After taking the Athens bus, he got off at the Stone Mountain stop. Two people approached him, waving a picture of the "Monument to All Mothers". They looked like a couple of ordinary visitors to the famous park. The man was of robust build and was wearing an Olympic boxing shirt; the woman was of slight posture wearing jeans and seemingly shy.

"I am sorry, Sir," said the woman as they approached him. "You did not have time to sign this picture at the Park. We are working for an organization fighting drug abuse;

perhaps after giving us your signature, you could add a few words of encouragement for our group?"

Ookk looked them straight in the eyes; both of them were wearing the Martian souvenirs pinned to their shirts.

"I will gladly do that, if you sign the petition supporting my project," he answered.

At this point, the woman became somewhat hesitant but replied resolutely:

"We will be happy to do that. Perhaps when you write, you could support the card on the back of our van standing nearby. It will be easier to write."

This sounded reasonable to Ookk. He proceeded to the van, after they opened the back door. He leaned forward to write the card on the floor of the van. This was the last thing that he remembered from the episode. He was hit with a rubber hammer on the back of the head and lost consciousness. Two men sitting inside the van pulled him in; the back door was slammed shut and the vehicle took off quickly, without anyone seeing the incident.

Ookk did not know for how long he had been driven. All he knew was that he was sitting in a hole in the ground, tightly bound with a heavy rope, his hands cuffed behind his back and his ankles in chains, with a gag in his mouth. The hole was not very deep and, because of his height, his head was sticking above the ground, covered with leaves and tree branches. As far as he could see through this cover, he was in a freshly-cut hay field; the smell of hay confirmed his impression. Beyond, there was a huge field with nothing else in sight except the edge of a forest on the far horizon. It was obvious to him that he was being held captive for some unknown reason.

Later in the evening, two men approached him; they bent over the hole in the ground, and the younger of the two addressed him:

"Don't you worry, Sir, you should be happy that you didn't die; we saved your life. You will stay here for a while, perfectly safe, unless you start moving. Then we would have to kill you. You can scream as much as you want, if you can; there is nobody for miles around to hear you. I will come every evening and feed you. It is warm so you won't catch a cold," he laughed. "Not a hair will be harmed on your head unless, as I said, you move. I am warning you! Help will come and if everything works out, you will be O.K – free to go to Mars!" he laughed again.

With these words, he bent over him and fed him some sort of broth, until he said he had enough. Ookk saw, in the meantime, the figure of the second man, standing on the side of the hole; he definitely was the same man he had met at the bus stop. Ookk wanted to ask his captor a question, but he put a finger to his lips.

"No talking, please. I better gag your mouth, just in-case."

Thereafter, he again put a gag in his mouth and they left. Ookk slept most of the night. He had a severe headache from being hit on the head; he still felt the bump when he leaned against the wall of the hole.

Early in the morning, he was awakened by birds flying around and picking on the freshly-cut twigs covering his head. "Birds bring good luck", he thought to himself, "that is what Uta says."

He had plenty of time to think. He did not believe that his captors would kill him. If they wanted to, for some unknown reason, they would have done so already. He was, obviously, taken for ransom. But he also realized that he could starve if no one paid the ransom, since nobody knew he had disappeared. Nobody was at the bus stop when he was abducted.

During the day, he moved only slightly as far as he could within the tied rope. There was nothing to do but think. All the events of the past few weeks crossed his mind: Stone Mountain Park, Uta, the Prutenian soccer team, Abercorn, Kostek, the trip with his plane to Atlanta, the meeting at the Evergreen Convention Centre, and the gelling process of the project of the "Monument to All Mothers". And now, at the height of his popularity, he may be gone forever! For a moment, he considered that people would think that he had returned to Mars, but then he remembered that his plane was still at Stone Mountain Park.

Ookk was dozing late in the evening when he heard the two men approaching his dugout again. They were talking between themselves in low voices, but it was a quiet evening and Ookk could hear their conversation.

"The stupid asses dug the hole too shallow, so that the head of the fool sticks above the ground like a sore thumb. It's good that nobody works in this field; the work is finished for the season", said the younger man.

The other man, whose voice Ookk recognized from the meeting at the bus stop, said something that was of great interest to him:

"I asked for only gold coins and jewellery, not paper money, because they mark it. As soon as we get it, we can take off and get rid of it slowly in Florida."

They stopped talking when they approached the prison hole where Ookk was pretending to be asleep.

"The asshole is asleep or maybe he fainted from the smell of his own crap", he laughed loudly. He leaned down, shook Ookk's head and took the gag out of his mouth.

"Hi, your Heavenly Highness", he said sarcastically, "have some broth; we don't want you to starve – not yet anyhow."

Upon which, he fed him again some kind of soup until Ookk signalled that he had enough. He was gagged again and they walked away. Ookk could hear their steps for quite a while. He thought that, after a few minutes, the sound of the walking changed from that of walking through grass to walking on a hard surface. "They must now be on a road", he thought.

Ookk's sudden disappearance caused a great deal of consternation in the Stone Mountain Camp. Actually, when he did not show up the first night, nobody paid much attention. Since Michael also had not returned, they thought that they had been invited by some important people to stay in Atlanta. The only person who had an uneasy feeling was Uta, but she did not say anything.

However, when Richard and Michael arrived in the morning with the Olympic bus and asked for Ookk, all hell broke loose. There were all sorts of theories, none of them sensible and, certainly, none of them corresponded to the truth.

"Ookk went back to New Mexico to return to Mars", proposed Jana.

"He would not leave me," said Uta, "I bet he is collecting more signatures at the Olympic Park, or on the streets of Atlanta, and we will see him tonight. Abercorn thought that he might have gotten lost in the woods again. "It is easy to get lost there among the damn old trees; I got lost once myself. The guy has no compass and he hasn't been around here for long", he commented.

Kostek suggested that he had gone to the Convention Centre to talk to Mr. Ericsson about organizing a meeting with the Atlanta business community, because he had mentioned to him that he was planning such a step.

In any case, the police at Stone Mountain Village were notified; this time the group had more credibility. Kostek suggested that Richard and Michael go to Atlanta and discuss his disappearance with the higher police authorities; Ookk was now known to many important people, including the Mayor and the officers of the Atlanta Olympic Committee.

"In the meantime, we should go and practice, instead of brooding. He will be found today, so why waste valuable time?" Kostek insisted.

Uta could not understand Kostek's attitude. How could she practice soccer, knowing that Ookk was lost? She blamed herself for not being with him all the time. Although she was recently estranged from Ookk, when he disappeared she realized how much he meant to her. However, Kostek's suggestion was logical. So they all walked to the soccer practice field, while Richard and Michael went with the Olympic bus to Atlanta to organize a search for Ookk.

Uta was unable to lead her team that day. Ookk was on her mind. "What am I doing here practicing, while my beloved is lost, perhaps is even in great danger?" she thought. Her teammates complained that she was not making any effort and, if things continued this way, they would lose the game.

"Uta, I know how you feel. It is better if you let Kostek arrange the plays and you just sit and relax", said Jana.

"I cannot relax and I cannot play," Uta replied.

Finally, since she was very impatient she decided that she should hitch hike on the freeway to Atlanta and wait for any message about Ookk in the newsroom of the Atlanta Journal. The soccer team continued to practice without Uta for the first time.

"That is what love does to people; they become restless and useless", concluded Kostek.

After arriving in Atlanta, Richard and Michael went immediately to the NBC Newsroom and told the manager about Ookk's disappearance. He was an experienced and compassionate man. He said that Ookk was most likely being held for ransom and, sooner or later, they will get a message about his whereabouts.

"I wonder where they could hold a guy that visible because of his height", he queried, "unless he is somewhere in the woods. I will make an announcement immediately that an extremely tall man has been kidnapped and that anyone who has any information should report it, or come to the station. We can include his picture in the telecast, but I would suggest that we don't say he is from Mars. Some people may interpret it as a joke. I think it's a good idea to invite people to come to the station; we can sort them out, to see who really has information and who just wants to appear on T.V."

He barely finished the sentence when Uta dashed into the conference room. She had not waited for a bus but hitchhiked to Atlanta. Naturally, she also thought that NBC was was a good medium to spread the news about Ookk's disappearance.

The manager invited Uta to stay at the station.

"If you wish, you can stay here with your friends, watch the news, and help us talk to the people who show up, because we are very busy running a news coverage station. Though I don't think we have to go that far with our message to find Ookk", he added jokingly.

It was decided that Michael and Uta should stay at the NBC news station. Richard wanted to explore things on his own. He always had a secret ambition to be a detective and this was a wonderful opportunity, he thought: to search for a man with the only available information being that he was extremely tall.

But more information soon became available. A note was found in the office of the State Botanical Garden of Georgia, at 2450 Milledge, in Athens.

The message was printed and addressed to the International Olympic Committee, saying:

"Ookk is in perfect health, well hidden, and waiting to be freed! If you deliver gold coins and jewellery worth a hundred thousand dollars, within 48 hours, he will be returned. Please leave a bag on the back wall of 170 North Finley Street in Athens. Do not place police around the area because if they catch us, your man will die. We are not asking much, but we mean business."

The note was typed on computer paper and the address was printed on the reverse. The officials of the Botanical Garden immediately notified State Police and the FBI. The note was not shown to anyone but the police told Michael and Richard about its content. Uta was informed about it in a milder form, being told just that Ookk, was safe and the police had a clue where to look for him. The T.V. stations, radio stations, and the newspapers all made a brief comment that a note had been received from Ookk's captors and that the FBI hoped that they had sufficient clues to find him. Actually, further publicity was overshadowed by the Olympic events, such as daily reports on competitions, medals and records. The festival mood of the city was so great that nothing could dampen it. At the Prutenian camp, there was an air of uneasiness all the time. Without Ookk's presence, life and soccer practices were not the same. Actually, Uta did not participate in the soccer games but accompanied Michael to his meetings with the police officials. Naturally, the police wanted to know more about Ookk's habits, his character, and endurance. Since they were closer to Ookk than anybody else, they could supply a lot of information vital for the investigation. "These things are important in any kidnapping case", they were told.

It was interesting how many people showed up at the T.V. station wanting to give information about Ookk. Most of them really meant well. Others were simply hoping to appear on T.V. Several people had seen Ookk taking the Stone Mountain Freeway bus, and confirmed that he got off at Stone Mountain Park. Unfortunately, nobody was present to identify the van in which he had been abducted. Actually, in the evening of the next day, an abandoned farm van was found near the Stone Mountain Village; as is the case with many farm vehicles, the van was not registered; if it were, it had to be from somewhere other than Georgia. Apparently, the whole ransom operation was well planned out and well executed, with a minimum of risk involved.

Since the note had been delivered to the office of the State Botanical Garden, the attention of the police authorities was centred on this huge horticultural preserve of some 300 acres, located on Route 441, south of Athens. The Botanical Garden, at this time of the year, was a busy place visited by thousands of people, because of its natural diversity: it had several miles of trails winding through different ecological systems and eleven gardens, devoted to many species of flowers.

After the note from Ookk's captors was delivered, the police closely watched all entrances to the Garden, without disturbing the visitors. In the meantime, several specially-trained crews were searching the Gardens for Ookk, so far without result.

Richard thought that the best way to proceed in his detective work was to follow the games he had played on his Sega video game. If the note from Ookk's abductors was delivered in Athens, he reasoned, Ookk had to be in this area. The delivery of the message to the Botanical Garden Office could be an intentional deception, to confuse the police by searching the Garden. In the meantime, he thought Ookk could die or the abductors could disappear.

Richard decided on a different search plan. He called up some twenty of his friends and asked them to get bicycles and to tour the agricultural roads around Athens: the bikers looked like people on an excursion and would not arouse any suspicion. No cars, no noise, he thought. They divided the area into six quadrants between Routes 78 West, 129, 441, 29, and 78 East, and started cycling during all the daylight hours, from dawn to dusk.

During the second night, Ookk could not sleep. The smell of his excretions was terrible. However, he was kept awake by a groundhog at his feet, which obviously had burrowed a tunnel from its cave to the hole where Ookk was sitting. A quick thought flashed through his mind: "I have to kill the groundhog". This was an unpleasant task but he did that, thumping his chained legs up and down until the groundhog was dead, its skin and intestines being split in the process.

Ookk's action was intentional. He noticed crows circling around looking for food in the freshly-cut hay field. "They will converge on my hole as soon as they smell the meat. Michael said that they always clean the highways of dead animals run over by cars", he thought to himself. Indeed, the crows swooped down in droves to the hole, picking up pieces of meat from the dead animal. The satisfied crows obviously signalled other crows about their finding. Soon, Ookk's "cave" was a source of attraction for hundreds of crows circling around and fighting amongst themselves, which was both noisy and spectacular. This scene, as was later revealed, was not too far from Route 78 East, close to the South Bypass, entering Broad Street, southeast of Athens.

One of Richard's friends, bicycling in the area, noticed the unusual aggregation of crows around the spot in the hay field. He spoke on his walkie-talkie to Richard, who was surveying the neighbouring region between Route 78 and 129.

"I will come over," answered Richard. "I hope it is not the body of Ookk that the crows are picking at."

He joined his friend John and they both walked from their bicycles on a gravel road into the hay field, where the crows were making a violent racket. They found Ookk sitting in the hole, exhausted but in good spirits. They immediately notified the police who were patrolling the Botanical Garden. An ambulance came to pick up Ookk, who was by then freed after Richard and John had cut the rope which bound him. They could not cut handcuffs or the chain on his legs so he was taken to the Athens University Hospital with the evidence intact. Ookk insisted that Richard travel with him in the ambulance, which apparently was against the rules. However, Ookk was so insistent that the ambulance driver had no choice but to permit Richard to join them. A detective also accompanied Ookk until his handcuffs were cut and he was comfortably deposited in the hospital bed for an interview concerning the identity of his abductors. The bed was too small and the frame had to be removed.

"Can you describe to me the people who abducted you", the FBI agent asked. "The more information you give us about the incident, the easier it will be for us to identify the gang."

Ookk described the man and his female companion who had abducted him at the Stone Mountain bus stop. He also described the van in which he was writing his autograph, and the hole in the hay field in which he was imprisoned. He also described the appearance of the young man who had come to feed him, and the conversation about the ransom which he had overheard the second evening.

The detective highly praised the way Ookk attracted attention by thinking of the crows as scavengers. He also congratulated Richard on his idea of surveying the area around Athens.

"The note referring to the Botanical Garden was obviously a diversionary tactic by the gang. We did observe the house on Finley Street in Athens, referred to in the ransom note, but we did not want to place any people there, in order not to jeopardize your life", he said to Ookk. "The area would have been difficult to police because it's close to a hotel."

"I thought that the people who abducted me were intelligent", Ookk said. "They did not ask for paper money, which could be marked. They reminded you not to survey the spot where the ransom would be deposited, threatening that I would be killed, and they did not ask for one million

239

dollars. Obviously, they hoped that the episode would be over promptly and they would get a considerable amount of money without any danger. Maybe I am superstitious but Uta, my friend, said that birds bring good luck. One did sit on my head. The birds saved my life", concluded Ookk.

Ookk was soon released from the hospital into the care of Uta and her friends at the Stone Mountain camp. He was lying comfortably in his hammock, reviewing with them his terrifying experience, while holding Uta's hand.

"You know, Uta, generally speaking, I am lucky! I met you. You found me in the Wildlife Trails, where I could have perished, and now I was found again unharmed."

The gang that abducted Ookk was never caught. When Ookk reported that they had a different accent, it was concluded that they were not Georgians. Local people would not do it to Ookk. He was their hero!

News of his release spread fast. For some people, it was the first news they heard of his disappearance. Again there were many press reports under various titles:

"Martian Captured by Earthians."

"Another Horror Story of Capture for Ransom. First in Georgia."

"Ookk Reunited with his Friends."

"The 'Monument to all Mothers' Project to Continue."

"Ookk Again on the Go."

***

CHAPTER 18

FOLLOWING Ookk's recovery after his ordeal during captivity, it was unanimously decided that the group should do some sight-seeing in Atlanta. Kostek, after assessing the "state of the art" of the soccer performance, fortunately agreed. They felt that one could miss a lot by not seeing Atlanta during the Olympics. Uta, particularly, wanted to renew her closeness to Ookk, which had cooled off during her intensive soccer practice. She thought that the sightseeing might give her the opportunity to do this. What suited her was the fact that the team members were given a free hand in going alone on city tours. Naturally, Ookk selected Uta as his companion.

Seeing Atlanta during the Games was not an easy task. It was the first time that the American South was presenting itself to the world as a place with a wide variety of activities, and not only as a business centre. Crowds of people literally flooded the parks and city streets. A staggering number of athletic and cultural events were taking place.

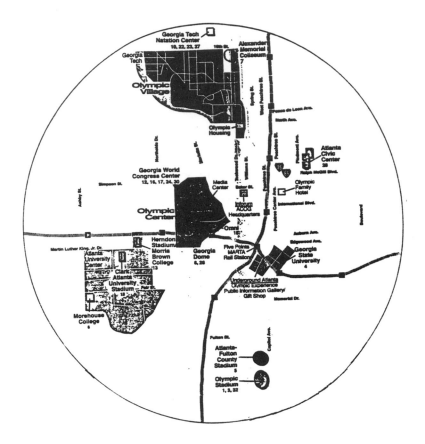

The Olympic Ring, an Imaginary Circle, 1½ miles in diameter which includes the principal locations of Olympic Events. All these Athletic Centers can be reached by MARTA

(Courtesy of Atlanta Committee for the Olympic Games)

After the Olympic Flame was brought from Greece and lit high over the Olympic Stadium, Atlanta became electrified: the big moment had finally arrived – after years of preparation, following the selection of Atlanta as the site of the Centennial Olympics. One hundred and seventy-six countries were participating in 32 sports competitions, ranging from Archery and Athletics to White Water Canoeing, Wrestling, and Yachting. Ookk and Uta were particularly interested in soccer, and the finals which would be held in the classic city of Athens. However, they wanted to get a grasp of other sports competitions; they promised each other to attend the next Winter Olympics as well. Ookk did not wear his Martian space suit for two reasons: it was too warm and he did not want to draw attention to himself. By now, many people recognized his towering figure. When he walked with Uta or attended some events, he was constantly stopped and asked for his autograph to be placed on books, tickets, shirts, sun umbrellas, or whatever the person was carrying. He was brazen enough to carry with him a book for signatures and addresses of people to elicit support for the "Monument to All Mothers"; the book was soon filled with names and addresses.

The main area of the Olympic activity was something called the Olympic Ring, an imaginary circle which included the principal locations: the Olympic Stadium, the adjacent Fulton County Stadium, the massive Olympic Centre with the Georgia World Congress Centre, the CNN Centre, the Georgia Dome and Omni, the Clark Atlanta University Stadium, and the Herndon Stadium. This imaginary Magic Ring, with a radius of about one and a half miles, had the advantage that all these Athletic Centres

PROGRAMME OF THE 1996 ATLANTA CENTENNIAL OLYMPIC GAMES *

Sport

1.	Opening Ceremony	Olympic Stadium	85,000
2.	Archery	Stone Mountain Archery Field	5,000
3.	Athletics (Track & Field)	Olympic Stadium	85.000
4.	Badminton	Georgia State University	5,000
5.	Baseball	Atlanta-Fulton County Stadium	50,000
6.	Basketball	Georgia Dome	25,000
		Morehouse College/Atlanta University Center	6,000
7.	Boxing	Alexander Memorial Coliseum	10,000
8.	Canoeing	Conyers, Rockdale County	20,000
9.	Cycling	Stone Mountain Velodrome	7,500
10.	Diving	Georgia Tech Natation Center	10,000
11.	Equestrian	Georgia International Horse Park	varies
12.	Fencing	Georgia World Congress Center	3,000
13.	Field Hockey	Herndon Stadium/Atlanta University Center	10,000
		Clark Stadium/Atlanta University Center	5,000
14.	Football (Soccer)	Sanford Stadium, Athens (semi & finals)	80,000
15.	Gymnastics	Omni	17,000
16.	Handball	Georgia World Congress Center	7,500
17.	Judo	Georgia World Congress Center	7,500
18.	Pentathlon	Various Sites	varies
19.	Rowing	Conyers, Rockdale County	20,000
20.	Shooting	Wold Creek Trap & Skeet Range	5,000
21.	Softball	To Be Determined	7,500
22.	Swimming	Georgia Tech Natation Center	15,000
23.	Synchronized Swimming	Georgia Tech Natation Center	10,000
24.	Table Tennis	Georgia World Congress Center	5,000
25.	Tennis	Stone Mountain Tennis Complex	12,000
26.	Volleyball	Georgia Dome	25,000
27.	Water Polo	Georgia Tech Natation Center	10,000
28.	Weightlifting	Atlanta Civic Center	4,500
29.	Whitewater Canoeing	Ocoee River, Tennessee	15,000
30.	Wrestling	Georgia World Congress Center	7,500
31.	Yachting	Atlantic Ocean, Savannah	varies
32.	Closing Ceremony	Olympic Stadium	85,000

* Courtesy of Atlanta Committee for the Olympic Games

Piedmont Park, and Mid-Town Atlanta

could be reached by MARTA. Uta thought first that it was named after a Marta – the first name frequently used in her native Prutenia- only later did she learn that it stood for Metropolitan Atlanta Rapid Transit System. It was indeed rapid: when they rode on the MARTA from the last bus station close to Stone Mountain Park it zoomed through the city at tremendous speed.

Naturally, Ookk and Uta were familiar with the sporting activities taking place at Stone Mountain Park: Archery, Cycling, and Tennis in the new beautiful Tennis Complex, equal to any other World Tennis Centre. When observing some of the events, Ookk's thoughts returned to the time when he had landed in the Wildlife Trails. The site of his landing was obviously not selected; he had seen a huge granite mountain from the air and landed on its slope. "Fate is fate", he thought, "if I had landed in some other place, I would have never met Uta". Her thoughts were actually going in the same direction, as it often happens between persons close to each other. She thought how fortunate she was that there was no room for her team at the Olympic Village; otherwise, she would never have met Ookk.

Some of the sports they could not attend because they were held out of town and there was not sufficient time to travel. Canoeing and Rowing were held at Conyers in Rockdale County, and Whitewater Canoeing on the Ocee River on the Tennessee State border. The Shooting competition was scheduled at Wolf Creek Trap and Skeet Range. Ookk insisted on making a list of all participating countries, promising himself that even if he could not visit them all, he would at least have their names for future reference.

It was, as usual, a warm summer. Any competition required endurance and, therefore, the athletes from countries where the weather was hot had an advantage simply because they were used to it. Some capacity to endure is inherent to sporting activities. Ookk did not see anything wrong with it. He asked Uta what happens when the Olympics are held in cold countries?

"Well", answered Uta, "then the situation is reversed; the athletes from hot countries are at a disadvantage."

It should be said that Atlanta did everything possible to diminish the effects of heat. Good drinking water was accessible to the public all over the city. Some cement structures in the stadiums were painted white; it was esthetically very pleasant and, at the same time, it diminished heat absorption.

One of the problems, for which improvements were suggested, was the overheating of stadiums, due to continuous solar radiation, as well as heat generated by the spectators, particularly when they were frequented by large crowds of 50-100,000 people for several hours. Theoretically, the creation of air movement by blowing, reduces heat. A different method was recently proposed by Dr. F. Van Zeggeren, a physical-chemist in Toronto, working with the Advanced Research Centre for Physical Sciences. He suggested that cooled air from outside the stadium could be introduced at the lower level which, consequently, would push the hot air upwards. By placing diffusors or baffles at the air receptors, the spectators would be only minimally affected by the draft. For instance, two dozen of duct outlets could be installed around the lower level at the periphery of

The High Museum of Art, Atlanta

the stadium; the total air input would amount to over one billion litres per hour, i.e. each pump having a capacity of about 20,000 cubic feet per minute. Such systems would be expensive but the cost/benefit ratio would be low, suggested Van Zeggeren.

Devices have also been tested to reduce temperature in outdoor arenas by spraying a mist above the surface and then blowing it away as it evaporates; this would create a type of air conditioning, lowering the temperature by 9^U. In any case, it is only fair to say that Atlanta did everything humanly possible to reduce adverse athletic conditions.

In addition to the events, Atlanta presented simultaneously a Cultural Olympiad by bringing well-known artists from other parts of the country, as well as from abroad. Atlanta has always had a wide range of cultural institutions, which served as focal points for the local arts community. The Woodruff Art Centre, located in downtown Atlanta, is a large institution combining both the visual and the performing arts; it consists of the Metropolitan Memorial Arts Building and the High Museum of Arts. The Centre is the home of the Atlanta Symphony Orchestra, the Alliance Theatre Company, and the Atlanta College of Art.

A second large centre is the Callanwolde Fine Arts Centre, located in a large Tudor-style mansion; Ookk met some of the students who were taking singing or dancing lessons at the Centre. Internationally known artists also presented their exhibits there. The Nexus Contemporary Art Centre offers an exchange program between artists and visitors, including gallery exhibits and artistic programs, in addition to housing the Nexus Press, which publishes works by artists in book form.

The Callanwolde Museum, Atlanta

There are other Centres which should be mentioned: the Soapstone Centre presenting exhibitions and performances by diverse ethnic groups, and the well-known Harry Bryce African-American Dance Theatre. Alternate Roots is an innovative regional cooperative which presents original works of the American Southeast.

Music was certainly well represented during the Olympics, including festivals such as Atlanta Jazz, the National Black Arts Festival, the Georgia Renaissance, A Taste of Atlanta, and Arts Live. A chamber-music ensemble, Atlanta Virtuosi, was once described by Henryk Szeryng as being "among the finest chamber groups of today."

There were numerous other cultural activities, such as the Atlanta Bach Choir performing an eighteenth-century repertoire in Latin or German; the Atlanta Singers; the Thamyris at Clayton State College; and the Southwestern Savoyards devoted to Gilbert and Sullivan.

Tara, who knew museology as well as music became particularly interested in the Centre for Puppetry and Arts, located in the renovated Museum. There were over 200 puppets representing different cultures and styles. The variety was indeed incredible. Puppets are very popular in Slavic countries, particularly the Puppet Theatre which permits satire on any governing system. In the Centre she could try to manipulate interactive puppets. She also saw Jim Hanson's video which showed the famous puppeteers around the world. Naturally, the traditional rustic puppets were well represented. What amazed Tara were the electronically mobile puppets including Hanson's "Pigs in Space" and those

The Coca-Cola Fountain, Atlanta

modeled after mythological figures. "If I stay in the U.S.A. perhaps I will open a puppet theatre", she thought to herself.

Ookk and Uta could not possibly visit all these Centres, but they went to some of them. Uta particularly enjoyed the Atlanta Opera and the Atlanta Chamber Players, performing works written for them by American composers. Ookk was interested in Jazz, Louis Armstrong style.

***

CHAPTER 19

OOKK remembered only too well that when he had been collecting signatures of supporters for his project at the Olympic Park, two officers from the Immigration Service had come to see him. They had asked Ookk to pay them a visit at the Immigration and Naturalization Assistance Office in Atlanta, after he had finished his presentations. They were polite and they knew that Ookk's activities had the approval of the city authorities, as well as the Atlanta Olympics Organizing Committee. Undoubtedly, they had also read articles about him in the Atlanta Journal.

At this point, Ookk's personal affairs were in good order. He had reconciled with Uta, realizing that they were meant for each other. They had decided to get married, but did not know when or where. This was obviously an opportune time to see the immigration officials. Ookk kept in the back of his mind the fact that if he were admitted as a resident of the United States and married Uta, she could stay with him. He decided to discuss the matter with her.

"Uta", he began one evening, "I was asked to clarify my immigration status. If we get married, and it looks like we will, you would have to stay with me after the members of your team go back to Prutenia?"

"You know very well, Ookk, that I could not desert all my friends. I am sure that if I were to ask the girls, some of them would also like to stay in the USA, if they're permitted to do so. How many athletes would refuse? Not many", she concluded.

"Well", replied Ookk, "apart from their wishes, this is a complicated question. The U.S. has complex immigration laws based on a 'country of birth quota system'. In this case, we have to act promptly if we want to be successful. I have already spoken to Jay Greenspoon as to whether he could find some way of sponsoring your friends. He would like to expand his operation and he is an inventive man. However, he cannot directly employ foreign visitors. Nevertheless, he is willing to come to the immigration hearing, if there is one. Perhaps, in the meantime, you can talk to the girls and I will speak to Jay once more."

Following this conversation, Uta held a meeting with her team members. She had learned that the girls were making their own plans. Richard was planning to sponsor Jana, and Michael had discussions with Sumita. Some of the other girls were talking to the members of the American Archery Team.

They were all anxious to join Ookk and Uta when they appear at the Immigration Assistance Office. Ookk called the office and was amazed that he received an extremely friendly reception and got an appointment for the next morning.

They all went there, dressed in their Prutenian Soccer Team uniforms, accompanied by Ookk. Richard, Michael, Kostek, and Abercorn joined them as observers. When they arrived, they noticed that the hearing room was full of curious people, including news reporters. Somehow, the word had leaked out that Ookk would be there, which was enough to bring out a crowd.

Before the hearing started, Ookk disappeared into the Immigration Judge's chamber for some twenty minutes. Nobody knew why and he didn't tell anyone whom he saw. He just told Uta that he wanted to talk privately to the judge, which she thought was unusual.

When the immigration judge entered the room, the proceedings began. The court clerk had Ookk, Uta and her team members, sworn in "to tell the truth and nothing but the truth." Ookk was the first to be called to the stand to explain his application as well as the mode of transportation he used on his arrival in Atlanta.

"Your Honour, I am flying an experimental plane and I have a licence for it. Actually, I arrived at Stone Mountain Park from New Mexico. I have permission from the City of Atlanta and the Federal Aviation Authorities to operate my aircraft."

"I did not know, Mr. Ookk, that you had arrived here from New Mexico. In that case, I don't have to concern myself how you arrived in New Mexico. You say that you have permission to operate your plane from the local authorities. I must say that you have done great things in Atlanta, including assistance to an injured athlete. I have also read that you want to help our city economically by building an educational facility in the Olympic Park?"

"You have my authority to become a citizen of the United States", he concluded.

When the judge finished his speech, there was complete silence for a moment. No one expected such a quick verdict; then the people in the room went into spontaneous applause.

"Hurrah, Ookk, Hurrah, Your Honour!"

After the noise subsided, the judge continued:

"I understand that you are planning to marry one Uta Fabian, a citizen from an area officially known as Dalmatia, who is visiting the United States with a soccer team, registered by the International Olympic Committee. She can obtain a U.S. Immigration Visa after she marries you. If any of her teammates wish to apply for immigration status, they will have to secure sponsors so that they will not be on the public charge. If they can obtain sponsors, I can waive the requirement for applying from outside the United States. May I have your answer to these questions?"

"Your Honour", replied Ookk. "I have previously contacted an Atlanta businessman, Mr. Jay Greenspoon, who is present in the audience. Would you permit Mr. Greenspoon to make a statement?"

Thereupon, the judge called Mr. Greenspoon to the stand, who after being sworn in, said:

"Your Honour, I own a souvenir factory in Atlanta. My business has become very successful because of the Olympic Games. I realized that people want to wear all sorts of souvenir pins and Mr. Ookk was very helpful in promoting my business. However, after the Olympics are finished, I have to think of how I can continue my business. As you know, unless I expand my business, the foreign competition will not allow me to make it profitable. The members of the soccer team from Prutenia by the way, I did not know that Prutenia was called Dalmatia before you said so, are all well educated in various professions, including engineering, architecture, biology, medicine, and music. This diversification would help my business because they know what sort of souvenir pins are required by members of their professions. I could employ them as consultants in my business."

"I see your point, Mr. Greenspoon", interrupted the judge. "I also believe that you have the financial resources to sponsor eleven people. However, we do not know how your business will develop. I would like to have some assurance that these girls, whether they live in Atlanta or elsewhere, have the means to support themselves. Are there any persons who could guarantee that they will not be on the public charge?"

In answer to the judge's question, at least thirty people in the room raised their hands. The judge was not joking. He asked the court clerk to record the names and addresses of all the volunteers, including their level of income. Among the volunteers were Richard and Michael, who wanted to vouch for Jana and Sumita respectively. However, at this point, they had only to register their names; they were happy that they did not have to submit their income level as they were both students. The persons who registered were mainly from Atlanta, because this was where the girls were known. Surprisingly, enough persons from other States, like California, Colorado, and Florida, also registered, including naturally Texas, Michael's birthplace. Jokes were flying around about "living together" as the people lined up for registration.

"You have to live with me for five years", Michael told Sumita.

"This is only a formality", she replied, "I might disappear on the first day, if you bother me."

After the registrations were completed, the judge gave all the applicants a working permit, with the proviso that they apply for an immigration visa, after securing a sponsor for a period of five years.

The hall was slowly emptying as the conversations continued about the future of the Prutenian team members and of Ookk. All agreed that this must have been the quickest immigration procedure in the history of the United States.

Since many reporters were present at the hearing, they took over the floor, interviewing the girls. The following conversation took place between Maria and a representative of the Atlanta Journal.

"I understand that you are a medical student. Do you realize that you will not be permitted to practice medicine in the United States? What are your plans?"

"My advantage is that I am young. I probably will have to repeat two clinical years in medical school. Our basic science education at the University of Zagreb is very good. The alternative is that I go back, graduate in Croatia, and return to the States. Then, I would have to take special examinations of the Educational Council for Foreign Medical graduates", replied Maria.

"Are these difficult?"

"They are very strict but, as I have said, if you have a good basic knowledge of medicine, it helps a great deal."

"Where would you practice?"

"I would like to do family practice or emergency surgery in the countryside. Even here in Georgia, there are many vacancies in remote locations.

Another reporter approached Tara.

"Excuse me, I cannot pronounce your last name, but your first name is Tara. How did you get such a "Georgian" name?

"My mother fell in love with the movie "Gone with the Wind". She wanted to call me 'Scarlet' in memory of Scarlet O'Hara, but that name would sound strange in our country; everybody would think of 'scarlet fever'. Tara sounded slavic, so I became 'Tara'."

"You are a musician by profession?"

"To correct you, I am a music student. But I am a composer and, in that field, talent counts. I think I am very good at it."

"Are any of your compositions known?"

"Perhaps not here. I wrote a very good melody called 'American Wedding March'. I will send you a copy when it is published in the United States. I hope it will be played at Uta's wedding."

"Anything else?"

"Yes, I wrote a melody for Atlanta on the occasion of the Olympic Games; I actually wrote it here. You have a fantastic city. I am sure you will like it."

"Can you whistle it for me?"

Upon which, Tara whistled the melody, "I can also give you the lyrics. It starts like this:

"I have travelled through
the many countries
Land and water on the way
Always hoping to see you
O, Atlanta...

Some people overheard the whistling and, soon, everybody was singing the new Atlanta song.

One of the visitors approached Tara, hearing her Atlanta song. He was a Japanese businessman, Yoshito Kitamura from the famous village of Tabuse, where his mother Ogamisama founded a new religion. He said, "I heard your melody for Atlanta. It is excellent! I've been away from Nippon for a while, travelling. I miss my country! Can you write for me a melody reflecting my longing for cherry tree blossoms, temples of Nara, Mount Fuji?"

Tara promised him to do it if he comes to their exhibition game in Athens. Apparently he did and got his song, "Bring me from Nippon..."

Another conversation concerned Jana and Richard. This was a reporter from the Atlanta Journal who had learned that Jana was in engineering and wanted to know more about the proposed "Monument to All Mothers".

"Tell me, if you construct a building in the form of a human body, which is of course not composed of straight lines, there would be many engineering problems. Can you tell our audience how you will approach that?"

Jana was ready for such a question, since she was asked about that many times previously.

"There are many problems, but they are not insolvable. The virtual reality program at Georgia Tech will be of great help because they can foresee the problems before the building is constructed. For instance, the surface could be composed of many triangle plates, to conform to a curved appearance, when the dimensions are large. If something goes wrong with one triangle, it can be replaced without demolishing the wall; in a sense, it is a modular construction."

"How about ventilation?", asked the reporter on the live TV show.

"This is very tricky because, in a sense, there will be many platforms to utilize maximally the space available. The building has to be well insulated, a process that is available through modern technology. The tricky question will be fire exits, which have to be designed so that they do not change the architectural appearance."

"I understand that your fiancé is a Canadian?"

"Yes. Richard is from Montreal. But that will give us an opportunity to meet a sculptor at the Univeristé de Montreal, Professor Pierre Grange."

"And then you will return to Atlanta to help with the design of the building?"

"I sincerely hope so! Perhaps Richard can play soccer for the Atlanta team?"

Everybody, who later saw Jana on the NBC News, thought that she performed very well, in spite of her accent.

***

264

CHAPTER 20

FINALLY, the big day came for the Prutenian team! The game against an American College Soccer Team which was arranged by the FIFA Committee to take place at the Georgia Coliseum of the University of Georgia at Athens. This sports and entertainment facility accommodates ten thousand people and the girls were surprised that such a large crowd arrived to see their exhibition game. However, they were by now well known in Atlanta, mainly through Ookk, who turned out to be a fantastic public relations agent.

Another piece of good luck was the fact that when they visited the FIFA Committee at the Butts-Mehre Heritage Hall, they met their old coach with a difficult last name: Pawlikaniec, called simply Kostek.

He introduced them to some new rules being proposed for consideration by FIFA. He insisted that there should be three referees covering the field, rather than one. In this way, lots of brutality was avoided because wherever the ball was, there was a referee to supervise the play and ensure fairness. In a sense, this also accelerated play because the time lost in deciding who was at fault was shortened due to the constant presence of a referee. Kostek showed them not only the tricks of playing good soccer but also introduced his plan of polyvalent training, in which each player apart from being in the attack in the middle or in defence was trained to play in all of the ten positions. He insisted that once a player got a yellow ticket he should be replaced as punishment rather than be allowed to continue to play. In this way, the players were not dead-tired from running on a field three times larger than that of hockey. He explained all his suggestions were very necessary, due to the fact that a women's team had to play against men; however, their games in Prutenia became very popular among the public not only because of more rapid action, but also because of fairness.

At this game, the rules that Kostek proposed proved to be of advantage to the Prutenian team. Since it was only an exhibition game, the American coach agreed to them, obviously underestimating the Prutenian girls' team. The disadvantage for them was the fact that they played on a perfectly maintained grass field, while in Prutenia, they played on dry solid surface. Consequently, moving the ball on the grass required much stronger hits. But the fact that Kostek trained with them for many days in Stone Mountain Park was of great help: all the tactical details which he taught them in Prutenia came back to Uta, who had taken over the coaching after Kostek left.

Naturally, Kostek came to their exhibition game, standing between Ookk and Uta and telling them constantly how to handle upcoming situations.

So they entered the field to the shouts of the excited public, announcements on the speakers, and loud music.

The American girls positioned themselves immediately in offensive positions and occupied the middle of the field in spite of Prutenian efforts. However, they were unable to break their concentrated grouping: this was Kostek's idea – with the extra running through the field, and the team's attack and defence, any attack of the opposing team became complicated. For the first few minutes, in spite of the fact that the defence remained intact, the ball went back to the Americans because the Prutenians misjudged the movement of the ball on the grass. The Americans tried then to shoot a long ball to the midfield from the margins of the field. The play remained static for quite a while until an American attack-player, Anita Jones, being frustrated by the inability to break the Prutenian defence, shot straight towards the Prutenian net. Jana, the strong Prutenian goalie, ran towards the ball, leaving the net. Her friend, Maria, did not see her and they collided; in the meantime, the ball slowly reached the empty goal. The public applauded loudly – the first, though unusual, American goal.

This shocked the Prutenians, and the Americans started to attack constantly, using the psychological advantage of their first goal. They were excellent in one-to-one encounters but the "triple security" tactic of Kostek limited them to somewhat uncoordinated attacks. The Prutenians also realized that they had nothing to lose and everything to gain by becoming more active. The Americans frequently fouled the play but each time this happened, one of the referees was there to observe and the player was exchanged. The way the Prutenians gradually got more encouragement from the public because of the way thet played; particularly Sumita, the centre attack player who used all sorts of gimmicks and avoidance schemes to keep the ball; finally, she tried to score from a distance of 20 feet, but hit the post. In the final five minutes of the first period, the Americans scored the second goal, after Wanda used her hand and fouled. She was removed from the field and Uta had to replace her, since the team did not have replacement players.

Kostek appeared depressed but realized that he had no alternative but to coach the team. Finally, he obviously could not hold himself back and started to berate Jana and the team as well. "Forget the play for results, just think of your home field and how you defeated so many men's teams – just do it again." He tried to tell them in an excited voice that their losses could still be reversed and that they should expend every effort at this point. They understood. This was the game of their life, this is why they had come to Athens.

The Prutenians returned to the field, somehow without their previous feelings of inferiority and embarrassment. They started their offensive play immediately. The public started to appreciate the lively play, giving frequent shouts and encouragement to players on both sides, whoever had the ball. The Americans scored another goal at the end of the second period which could not be defended by Jana.

In soccer matches, occasionally small events unrelated to the play change further events. After an attack of the left wing of the Prutenians, the ball landed close to the flag post.

The American player, Brenda, tried to stop the ball but as a result of her action, the flag post fell uprooting the grass. Maria, of the Prutenian team, who was close by, quickly straightened out the flag post and repaired the grass around it before kicking the ball. This polite action gained a prolonged applause from the public which, from then on, seemed to side with the Prutenians. At this point, Kostek decided to go into full attack by moving a fourth person, Maria, from the "midi" to attack position. The Prutenians continued to attack. Finally, Maria passed a long ball to Sumita, who scored a goal. This encouraged the Prutenian team. Shortly afterwards, Maria scored a second goal which turned out to be most spectacular.

Following two runs to the right wing, Sumita was running once again, this time with an American at her back: fortunately, she lost her with a skillful move and tried to pass the ball to Maria. As the ball was rolling, Dorothy, the American goalie, stepped forward a few feet from the net to catch it. Maria, with a swift move, got to the ball first: seizing the opportunity, she shot and scored! There was a general prolonged applause – the Prutenian girls were elated – and the score was equalized. The Prutenian girls could not contain their happiness; even to be playing against an American team was something they had never expected to achieve. They fell into each other's arms, kissed each other and cried.

The third period continued, as endless American attacks were repulsed by the Prutenians who, several times, kicked the ball out of bounds. The referees carefully followed all plays, noticing every foul and punishing it, thus leading to frequent exchanges of players. The play ended in a 3:3 tie.

The Prutenians seemed to be completely exhausted. Lying on the grass, they hardly heard the cheering public which, obviously, declared it to be best soccer game of the Olympics. Slowly, they realized that scores of reporters wanted to talk to them, so they moved to the bench, happy to see a beaming Kostek, they really played for him; they could not disappoint their old coach. they were not the only ones to cry – Kostek did too, probably for the first time in his life!

The excitement of the public was incredible. All of the members of the American College Team came over to the Prutenian girls to congratulate them on their effort. They all wanted to learn the new ways of handling the ball. Kostek got an offer to become their coach since, at the time, it was Uta and not him who was coaching the Prutenian team. The reporters were also waiting to interview him.

Some of the reporters asked Kostek about the rules of soccer used in this game. He explained them succinctly, giving his reasons for the changes he had proposed.

"Soccer, as it is played today, is too slow. The field is huge and the players get too tired running around. It becomes an exercise in endurance rather than ability to handle the ball."

"But endurance is important", interjected one of the reporters.

"Yes, but when the weather is particulary hot, it is exhausting and the result is that, compared to hockey, only a few goals are scored. The public likes to see action and when a player who fouls gets a yellow ticket, is changed, the new player is not tired because she is fresh."

"You mean that instead of being allowed to change only two players, all players could be changed, if at fault?"

"Exactly", answered Kostek, "this accelerates the play."

"What effect does it have on the public?" asked another reporter.

"They love it. The public loves a fast game. That is what they come to watch. It also gives the players a chance to show their skills."

"You also mentioned that having three referees instead of one decreases brutality. Couldn't the sideliners fulfil this function?"

"Perhaps, if they could do both: observe the line and judge at the same time which is not their job."

"Wouldn't it be more expensive to hire more referees?"

"It would, but it would pay dividends in safety and fairness of the play. You see, any brutality on the field is observed by the public; they react to it, sometimes by starting riots. You see this in some of the European games. It stops being a sport."

There were many FIFA officials among the public, and some of them, observing this game, certainly became aware of possible advantages of Kostek's proposals.

The game was surely a cause for celebration for both sides. The Americans invited the whole Prutenian team to the City Bar on College Avenue. Later, they made the rounds of all the well-known entertainment places, including the Frap Point Lounge of the Ramada Inn, the Ginkgo Tree Lounge at Holiday Inn, the Globe, and the Road House on Lumpkin Street.

When word spread among the American players that their new friends the Prutenians, had obtained work permits in the United States, there was jubilation anew with offers to join different teams.

Needless to say, apart from Kostek, for whom this was a great day, Richard and Michael were happy for Jana and Sumita, as well as Maria, who were the heroes of the day.

Ookk observed all this, holding Uta's hand tightly; they were so absorbed in each another that they were almost isolated from all the excitement.

***

CHAPTER 21

SINCE Uta and Ookk had decided to get married immediately after the end of the Olympic Games, they realized that endless preparations had to be made; perhaps more so because of the complex problems involved. A Martian getting married to a human being? It looked like it would be the wedding of the year, if not the century.

The first question was where and how to have the wedding. Uta was a Catholic, and Ookk was not baptized. She went to see the local priest in Athens and asked him whether he could perform the ceremony.

"You have to have permission from the Vatican. We have never had a case like this!"

"But God created the Universe", replied Uta, "and that includes Mars. Why can't a Martian be baptized if he wants to?"

"I am not saying he cannot be baptized. But I have to have permission from the Vatican, our highest authority. I don't believe that even the Archbishop of Atlanta could decide this question!"

At this point, Ookk asked the priest if he could speak to him privately. He took him into his room while Uta waited outside. They had a long conversation. Uta could hear excited voices through the door, but could not make out the words. She was happy when they emerged smiling.

"I cannot give you any details of our conversation since it was like a confession, but I have agreed to baptize Ookk as a special case."

Uta was overjoyed when she heard the news.

Ookk took the names of John Paul in honour of Pope John Paul II, since they do not have first names on Mars.

The arrangements were made immediately and Ookk became John Paul Ookk at a brief ceremony at the church in Athens. Jana agreed to become his godmother and Richard his godfather since both of them were Catholic.

There was no time to lose. Athens was selected as the site for the wedding ceremony. Since the Sanford Stadium could hold eighty thousand people and they did not know how many guests to expect, the site looked like a suitable location. Mayor O'Looney gave them her permission. It was also a question of expense, and the fact that all the Atlanta facilities were booked to capacity. Another advantage was that Uta and Ookk wanted to arrive in their plane, so they could land at Sanford after the guests assembled.

Athens was a friendly town, and thus the ceremony would be more in line with a big wedding in a small town;

that is what Uta thought because she had been brought up in a small town. Both she and Ookk liked Athens, so they were both happy about their choice; this is where the great exhibition game had been played, in front of thousands.

"After all", Uta thought to herself, "Athens was named after the birthplace of the Olympic Games. Could I think of a better place to get married? I can tell my friends that I got married one hundred years after the Games had started, and that I was married in Athens, Georgia, the site of the Soccer Olympics!" That idea appealed to her; like most girls, she was sentimental, particularly when getting married.

The next question that came up was who would be invited? They did not want to omit anyone and the number of people they met in Atlanta was countless. Ookk was just thinking of all the people he exchanged pins with, as a member of the Olympic Pin Club. Then he thought of the people from NASA, since he felt close to them. At least, they sent Viking probes to Mars. It is too bad, he thought to himself, that they did not explore the equatorial rift – if they had, they would have discovered that there is an atmosphere inside Mars with plants and humanoid life!

"The number of people who are going to attend the wedding is like a stochastic game", announced Jana.

"What does 'stochastic' mean?", asked Richard.

That word got them involved in a long conversation, since Jana loved to explain things.

"Aha", she replied, "you think that since I am from Prutenia, I don't know mathematics!"

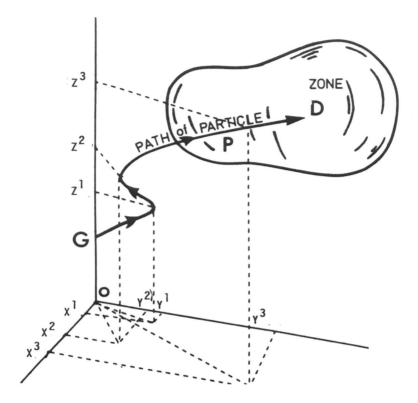

Diagrammatic presentation of operation of contributory factors in cancer development, none of which lead to cancer when present alone. In case of a stomach cancer the 'predisposing' factors which may be considered are: pernicious anemia (vector X), presence of a stomach ulcer (vector Y), familial predisposition (vector Z). These factors must operate at the same time in order to lead to cancer development (critical cancer zone D).

"No, seriously, I never heard of the word, nor has Michael."

"You see, Richard, our schools are very good in mathematics. Stochastics are chance mechanisms, in which the probability of occurrence can be calculated mathematically, if you know all the factors involved: a non-linear chance mechanism. Jerry Neyman, a professor of statistics at Stanford University in San Francisco, developed stochastic models for launching of space missiles, for agriculture, and many other fields. The point is that to propose a model, you have to know the extent to which participatory factors are involved in producing the 'final cause' (as defined by Maynard Keynes). These factors are always numerous and, frequently, not all of them can be identified; then the model is incomplete."

"These are 'Markov processes'. People frequently think that they have found something new, while in reality, there is nothing new under the sun!"

"Who was Markov"? A Russian General?", asked Richard.

"No, a Russian mathematician who developed the concept."

"Well", said Richard, "to me, this sounds like the Austrian weather forecast, which typically goes: 'It will be sunny unless there is rain'. I saw this prediction in a newspaper in Vienna. It depends on the amount of cloud."

"This is what it is", said Jana, "Weather prediction is very difficult because we do not know all the factors participating in creating weather."

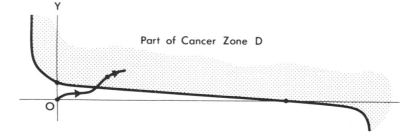

Diagrammatic presentation of a dominant causative factor in cancer development such as a carcinogenic chemical (Vector Y). If the resistance of the organism (Vector X) is low, a small development of Y vector will lead to cancer development (critical cancer zone D).

Richard and Michael were amazed by Jana's knowledge.

"Tell me one more thing, Jana", said Richard, "I am going to take advanced biology next year. Can you apply your stochastic theory to biology?"

"It is not my theory! It is Neyman's", replied Jana. "It is very difficult because many of the participatory factors are unknown. A Canadian scientist, Stanley Skoryna, applied it to the causation of stomach ulcers in 1963. He said that most people who have high stomach acid do not develop ulcers; nor do most people, who have a low resistance of the surface of the stomach to acid, develop ulcers: there must be several factors involved in ulcer development, otherwise stomach ulcers would be much more frequent."

"Such as what?", asked Michael.

"For instance, how much saliva you swallow per day, how fast your stomach empties, and newly discovered factors such as Helicobacter infection. He called them 'gastric let' mechanisms. 'Let' is an old English word implying hindrance – hindrance to develop ulcers."

"Is it like the 'Third Man' in the Viennese movie?"

"In a sense – the third, fourth, or fifth man. The point is that these mechanisms are non-linear. People who tried to make them linear have failed", Jana replied.

"Give me an example!"

"A good example is cancer in which causation is an incomplete stochastic model. For a long time, people thought that cancer develops by steps from nothing. Only

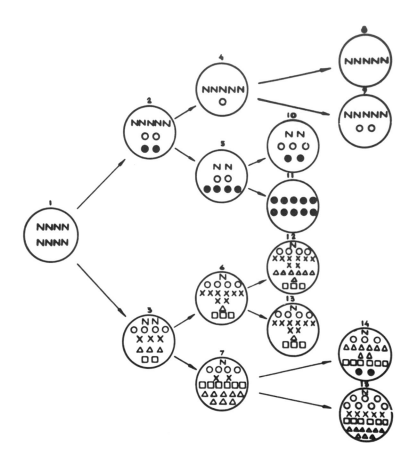

Diagram of different 'malignant' properties of cancer
cells which may occur in the same type of cancer:
N = Normal properties
O = High rate of growth
X = Invasion of surrounding tissue
Δ = Loss of differentiation of cells
□ = Spread to other locations (Metastases)
• = Local and systemic reactions against cancer
(immune responses)

now, do they realize that many factors participate in cancer development, acting at the same time," said Jana. "Cancer can develop from one cause such as a massive dose of chemicals but in most cases there is evidence of multiple participatory causation."

"That sounds logical! but is cancer not caused by genetic predisposition? Give me another example", Michael asked.

"Partly, take breast cancer in women, something everybody talks about. The genetic factor has been identified in 10% of women developing breast cancer. How about the remaining 90%? There are other known factors such as hormone levels, breast injury sustained during sexual activity, age, and perhaps psychological factors!, Jana continued.

"What you're saying is that in common cancers such as breast cancer, stomach cancer, or prostate cancer, several factors participate in cancer formation, naturally in addition to genetic predisposition. On the other hand we know that a severe exposure to a chemical or a large dose of radiation causes cancer without any additional factors. How do you reconcile these two theories?" asked Richard.

"The beauty or logic of the stochastic theory of Neyman is that it recognizes single causeative mechanisms such as exposure to chemical carcinogens or radiation as well as those of multi-coordinate type. A good example of single causation in human carcinogenesis is lung cancer developing very frequently in tobacco smokers. Good examples of multi-coordinate causations are cancers of breast, stomach, and prostate. Naturally the causative fac-

281

tors in each type of cancer are different. Another interesting phenomenon, according to Maria, is the inhibition of cancer spread by cancer already spread to the bones. Apparently when cancer of the prostate or breast is already spread to the bones, these people live much longer, even for many years without any treatment; others with cancer spread to soft tissues die much sooner. Perhaps some process occurs in bone remodelling which kills the cancer cells circulating in the blood. Nobody knows what this process is", answered Jana.

"Oh", exclaimed Richard, "I have read that President Mitterand of France lived for fourteen years with his cancer of the prostate which was spread to the bones. Now I understand that he actually had been protected by the presence of cancer in the bone tissues! Since you are so knowledgeable perhaps you could also tell me about causation of alcoholism; not only do I find you smart but I love to listen to your voice!"

"I am not a doctor; most of my information comes from Maria!", Jana replied. "Alcohol is a good example how some substances in small quantities have a positive effect on the human body, and a negative effect in large quantities. Alcohol in small amounts stimulates the human brain, that is why we call it 'spirits'. In large amounts, it causes liver and brain damage".

"But do these people have to drink?"

"They don't have to, but they want to when they become addicted. People from alcoholic families have a higher tendency to become addicted. But if their environment is not conducive to drinking, they will not become alcoholics even if both their parents were alcoholics. This is where the other factors participating in chronic alcoholism become important."

"What do you mean?"

"If you get depressed, because you lost your job, or if you suffer from chronic anxiety, meaning worrying about things without reason, then you are more likely to start drinking heavily."

"You got the point! We were talking about chance mechanisms involved in wedding invitations", Uta interrupted their conversation. She did not want to be impolite, but she realized that lots of problems had to be solved.

"Well", said Jana. "Your wedding was announced on the radio and TV News in Atlanta. Ookk was interviewed on television on NBC Network. Many people may show up only because of curiosity. We have sent invitations to all the important people, so that no one gets offended. But how many thousands will show up, we don't know. This is your stochastic mechanism."

At this point, they were happy that the wedding was taking place at the Sanford Stadium. It did not matter how many people would show up. Everybody was asked to bring their own "dinner basket" since there was no question of catering. A great contribution was made to the wedding by the Georgian wine growers. The industry, which had recently experienced a revival with an excellent Chardonnay, promised to donate one bottle for everyone who showed up.

"I wonder", Uta thought to herself, "whether they miscalculated the number of people who might come, it could be thousands. On the other hand, who will drive to Athens to get a bottle of wine? All that the people want to see is the first Martian get married on earth. But they will see me with Ookk! I will also be the attraction", she consoled herself.

There was undoubtedly some amount of anxiety among the citizens of Athens, with respect to the proposed wedding. Would crowds descend on Athens? Fortunately, the Mayor of Athens, Gwen O'Looney, was on the side of the young couple. She explained to the Council that the wedding would increase the number of tourists coming later to Athens, just to see where a Martian got married.

They were happy that the Mayor would attend the wedding reception. All this was arranged by Muriel Pritchett, Director of Services in Media Relations for Athens. She was quite worried about the press attendance, not that they would be few in number, but too many. At one of the meetings with Uta, she brought a local newspaper with articles about Ookk and Uta. The titles read as follows:

"Ookk to Marry Prutenian Soccer Coach."

"Athens to be Declared Soccer Capital of U.S.A."

"Monument for All Mothers' Proposed by Ookk for Olympic Centennial Park."

And then, it went on:

"Ookk Helps Transport a Patient with a Broken hip to the Emergency centre."

"The Exhibition Soccer Game Ends in a Tie Between Prutenia and the U.S. College Team: A Great Surprise."

With this sort of publicity, thousands of reporters were expected.

"I hope they report everything accurately", Uta thought.

***

CHAPTER 22

FINALLY, the grand day for Ookk and Uta arrived: a glorious August day for their wedding at Stanford Stadium in Athens. Uta's plan for a wedding at the Taylor-Grady Antebellum mansion was thwarted, because they were unable to predict the number of guests expected. However, when their SURSUM Skycar landed in the stadium field, she was happy to see thousands of spectators cheering wildly at their arrival. It was a colourful crowd, very international; many athletes were dressed in their national sports attire. There were also people from Atlanta, Athens, and the Stone Mountain Village.

The young couple were dressed in their soccer uniforms, as were Uta's bridesmaids who were her teammates, headed by Jana. Richard was Ookk's best man and Michael was in charge of the ushers. The wedding ceremony was necessarily brief because the stadium was to be used for one of the games. An altar was set up in the middle of the

The Sanford Stadium, University of Georgia, Athens

stadium field and a priest from a local church married them after a short mass. Uta could not hold back her tears when she heard the American Wedding March, composed by Tara for this occasion.

Ookk's thoughts travelled back to the day when he met Uta at the Stone Mountain Park. He wondered when he should tell her "the whole truth and nothing but the truth" – obviously, after the wedding. What will be her reaction? Will she accept him for what he is?

He realized that since they were both professionals, he would have to meet her objectives at least half-way and, preferably, more than half-way. He wondered whether a compromise could be achieved and whether their deep feelings will be sustained when faced with the problems of everyday life. However, on the whole, he was optimistic because he knew that their personalities were compatible. He recalled that their argument, as to the priority of soccer practice versus his plans to proceed with the building of the Monument to All Mothers, was resolved by the wisdom of his decision. "I must remember this lesson for the future", he concluded.

After the ceremony, Michael and the ushers led Ookk and Uta through the aisles to meet all the wellwishers. They were happy to see many prominent people among the guests, including President Samaranch, Dr. Havelange, and Mayors Billy Graham and Gwen O'Looney. In the crowd, they recognized their friends from the meetings at the Evergreen Convention Centre: Jim Babcock, Brent Ericsson, Bill Crane, Scott Mace, Nancy Nolan, Muriel Pritchett, and Abercorn Smith.

Everybody wanted to shake their hands and they were indeed fortunate that they were not mobbed. While the guests celebrated on Coca-Cola and Georgian Wine, Michael stepped up to the microphone and made a short speech.

"Ladies and gentlemen, we wish to thank you all for attending Ookk's and Uta's wedding which is also a celebration of Olympic friendship. While you continue to enjoy yourselves, I wish to announce that the young couple will now depart on Alpha Airlines on their honeymoon journey to Athens, Greece. This trip "from Athens to Athens" was made possible through the generosity of Alpha Airlines. I have just received the confirmation. As you all know, they will be headquartered in Atlanta and flies passengers all over the world from our fantastic city. We are all grateful to them for their generosity."

Upon which, and to the general applause of the guests, Ookk and Uta mounted their plane and soon disappeared over the skies of Athens, Georgia.

EPILOGUE

OOKK and Uta were sitting in Business Class of the Alpha Airplane going to Athens, this time the capital of Grecce. It was a night flight and they were both sleeping, holding hands.

When they woke up, a sumptuous breakfast was served. There was to be a stop and change of planes in Frankfurt, Germany. Since they still had almost three hours before landing in Athens, Ookk decided to tell Uta his biggest secret.

"Uta", he began, "now that you are my wife, I must tell you all my secrets. I was not born on Mars!" Ookk expected a shocked expression on her face, but instead, he was met with a complete lack of surprise.

"I am not surprised", answered Uta. "The first inkling I got that you must be an American was at the U.S. Immigration Office in Atlanta. The judge suddenly declared you to be an American citizen, after you went to see him in his chambers. I didn't want to say anything, but it certainly was surprising. I don't think anybody else noticed it. Then, when we asked to get you baptized in the Catholic faith, you went to see the priest and he withdrew his insistance on obtaining permission from the Vatican. I am from Prutenia and we think that anything is possible in America. Until these events occurred, I sincerely believed you for a long time and so did the others. But, tell me your story! What is your real name?"

"Now my real name is Ookk. I changed it before going to Atlanta. But, I shall start at the beginning. I am a scientist by profession and, actually, I have two doctorates: in Medicine and in Biology. It is indeed a long story. Since we have more than two hours before landing in Athens, I may as well tell it to you now.

"I was born and raised in the City of Beaumont, an industrial town in Southeastern Texas, located at the head of navigation on the Neches River. I studied at the local university of Lamar; later I studied for my doctorates at Houston's A&M University, which is only some eighty miles away.

"Being a very tall child, I was sort of isolated and certainly different from my classmates. I was always a problem. I remember my parents searching for 'extra-tall' clothing and 'extra-large' shoes. These difficulties were sometimes insurmountable and my clothing had to be made to measure. Fortunately, my parents were both professionals and I was their only child, so there were no financial problems. I didn't have to compete with any brothers or sisters.

In reality, I was brought up by nannies, who sympathized with me because of my height. You can imagine a very tall youngster, shy towards playmates and later towards girls, who was told that he is too tall for them. By the way, my mother, Mara, was also very tall but I outgrew her by far.

"My mother was a very energetic and autocratic person. She always told me and my father what to do and when to do it. She meant well and directed my education, but I always had the feeling that I had to listen to her, whether she was right or wrong. I wanted to do things on my own but was unable to do so.

"As I mentioned, I received doctorates in medicine and in biology, but I was constantly interested in other fields of endeavour: in architecture, in music, in engineering; I had an insatiable curiosity. In my graduate studies, I participated in all sorts of projects, naturally with my mother's approval, though I knew that she never liked my eclectic activities. One day, she took me to a neurologist, whom I actually knew professionally; he told her that I had a 'schizophrenic' personality. She did not tell me that. However, after this visit, my mother treated me differently; she treated me like a sick person.

"This is when our family relationship deteriorated. I was in Houston and visited my home less and less often. At that time, I was interested in space travel. I read extensively about the solar system, particularly about Mars and the 'Voyageur' probes. I also started flying, though I realized that ordinary planes were simply too small for me. I learned that a new type of 'bladeless' helicopter was being developed by Dr. Moller in Davis, California. I went to see him and fell in love with his new Skycar, because it allowed me to travel from point-to-point without going to the airport. It was difficult to obtain a license for this experimental plane, but I finally got it, with the proviso that I would not fly in Houston or any city in Texas.

"I always follow all rules and I followed them this time. I flew to the New Mexico desert; there was a lot of room there to practice flying in my new skycar.

"This was the time when my real story began. There's a small town in Texas, El Paso, on the border of New Mexico. Usually, I left my plane in a garage out of town and walked to a small hotel in the city. Naturally, everybody knew me there as a strange character, since I was always taciturn. In the hotel, they had to extend the frame of my bed to accommodate my height. So I was again an oddity." Ookk laughed at this point.

"I remember clearly the evening when it occurred to me that I could be a Martian. I was taller than anybody else and I thought that, perhaps, I belonged to Mars where everybody is of my height. As a doctor, I knew that this was not true but I had daily hallucinations that I came from Mars and that I am only visiting Earth. I started to believe in it. My delusions increased in severity to the extent that I bought some material to make a 'Martian suit' and I bought a special large helmet. This is how I imagined the Martians were dressed. I donned this suit every time I went to fly and when people on the street asked me where I was going, I simply answered that I am going to fly to Mars. In the El Paso hotel, people thought that I was crazy anyhow!"

The new version of Moller's skycar

"These were great times. I was admired by everybody in town. Some people thought I was mentally ill, while others believed that I was practising for some sort of a show: dressed in a skin-tight green uniform with an oversize helmet on my head. I must say that I enjoyed my role thoroughly. For the first time in my life, I was able to do anything I wanted, unhindered, and not advised by my mother.

The next episode occurred on July 4, 1996. I read in the local newspaper about the Centennial Olympics which were being held in Atlanta. How would it be, I thought, if I flew over and saw the Olympics as a Martian. Certainly, this would be a different point of view if I presented myself as a Martian, visiting 'Earth' for the first time. I had read extensively about Mars in the previous month and had not only specific knowledge about Martian topography, but also a good general education to answer intelligently any questions. The interesting thing about this episode was that I sort of knew that I was not a Martian, but I felt that I should play this role of bizarre behaviour in order to convince people that I was an extraterrestrial being. In effect, these were schizophrenic symptoms. Perhaps, the neurologist who examined me was right that I had a schizophrenic personality.

"You know the rest of my story after my landing at the Stone Mountain Park. Uta, you are the person that cured me! Finally, I met somebody with whom I want to spend a normal life."

"Ookk, but how were you able to imitate all the happenings supposedly taking place on Mars? Your

Group portrait of the original medical family.
Upper row: Apollo and Coronis; *Middle row:* Chiron,
Epione, wife of Aesculapius, Aesculapius; other wifes:
Arsinoe, Hippone, Xanthe and Aigle. *Bottom row:*
Machaon, Podalirius, Hygiea, Panacea, Iaso
and Aceso.

descriptions were so vivid that I dreamed of being on Mars!", Uta answered. She was now very excited, like a soldier after a battle. "Well, as you said, you studied a lot and you have a great deal of imagination. When you played the role of a Martian, you developed some sort of a split personality; as you admitted, for a while you believed that you were from Mars. As you know, your capture by the gang was real and I thought that I would never see you again! You risked your life. Thank God for your tremendous endurance!"

"When we are in Greece perhaps we could visit the Olympus, a mountain range in Thessaly, near the coast of the Gulf of Salonika" suggested Uta. "In ancient mythology this was the home of the gods. Since you are a doctor you may want to see the original medical family, Apollo and Coronis, Aesculapius and their sons. Podalirius the internist and Machaon the first surgeon."

"Uta, I feel so good with you on Earth and I do not need to go to Heaven! Imagine that I was on Mars and one heavenly voyage is enough for me!"

"You were certainly lucky to meet Dr. Moller and to get his Skycar, which you call Sursum. It is so different that it certainly was a hit with the public; it convinced them that you were not from this planet! What are you plans now? Where will we be living? Not on Mars, I hope!"

"For a while I would like us to go to Texas, to see my parents. I have already telephoned them from the Airport. I told them I will be bringing my wife with me. They were surprised, but not shocked. Nothing shocks them, after all the things I've done!"

"You are unbelievable! I hope they will like me. We also have to travel to Dalmatia so you can meet my parents. They will be happy to see me married. They thought I would never marry and play soccer! However, what do you want to do with your profession?"

"I can do many things, but as I have told you, before I do anything else, I want to build a 'MONUMENT TO ALL MOTHERS'.

*** THE END ***

ACKNOWLEDGEMENTS

The author wishes to thank the following organizations for supplying publications and information or inspiration for the material in this book.

Advance Research Corporation, Yardley, PA
Athens Convention and Visitors Bureau
Atlanta Chamber of Commerce
Atlanta Convention and Visitors Bureau
Atlanta Committee for Olympic Games
Atlanta Journal & Constitution, Atlanta, GA
Forward Atlanta, Atlanta, GA
Georgia Council for International Visitors
International Olympic Committee
Metro Atlanta Rapid Transportation System
Moller International Inc., Davis, CA
National Broadcasting Company, Atlanta, GA
Norian Skeletal Repair System, Cupertino, CA
Southern Bell, Atlanta, GA
Stone Mountain Park of Georgia Inc.
Turner Broadcasting System, Atlanta, GA

ADDENDUM

NATIONAL OLYMPIC COMMITTEES RECOGNIZED BY
THE INTERNATIONAL OLYMPIC COMMITTEE

AFG	Afghanistan	BOT	Botswana
ALB	Albania	BRA	Brazil
ALG	Algeria	IVB	British Virgin Islands
ASA	American Samoa	BRU	Brunei Darussalam
AND	Andorra	BUL	Bulgaria
ANG	Angola	BUR	Burkina Faso
ANT	Antigua and Barbuda	BDI	Burundi
ARG	Argentina	CAM	Cambodia
ARM	Armenia	CMR	Cameroon
ARU	Aruba	CAN	Canada
AUS	Australia	CPV	Cape Verde
AUT	Austria	CAY	Cayman Islands
AZE	Azerbaijan	CAF	Central African Republic
BAH	Bahamas	CHA	Chad
BRN	Bahrain	CHI	Chile
BAN	Bangladesh	TPE	Chinese Taipei
BAR	Barbados	COL	Colombia
BLR	Belarus	COM	Comoros
BEL	Belgium	CGO	Congo
BIZ	Belize	COK	Cook Islands
BEN	Benin	CRC	Costa Rica
BER	Bermuda	CIV	Côte d'Ivoire
BHU	Bhutan	CRO	Croatia
BOL	Bolivia	CUB	Cuba
BIH	Bosnia and Herzegovina	CYP	Cyprus

NATIONAL OLYMPIC COMMITTEES RECOGNIZED BY
THE INTERNATIONAL OLYMPIC COMMITTEE

CZE	Czech Republic	GUA	Guatemala
DAL	Dalmatia*	GUI	Guinea
DEN	Denmark	GUY	Guyana
DJI	Djibouti	HAI	Haiti
DMA	Dominica	HON	Honduras
DOM	Dominican Republic	HKG	Hong Kong
ECU	Ecuador	HUN	Hungary
EGY	Egypt	ISL	Iceland
ESA	El Salvador	IND	India
GEQ	Equatorial Guinea	INA	Indonesia
EST	Estonia	IRQ	Iraq
ETH	Ethiopia	IRL	Ireland
FIJ	Fiji	IRI	Islamic Republic of Iran
FIN	Finland	ISR	Israel
FRA	France	ITA	Italy
GAB	Gabon	JAM	Jamaica
GAM	Gambia	JPN	Japan
GEO	Georgia	JOR	Jordan
GER	Germany	KAZ	Kazakhstan
GHA	Ghana	KEN	Kenya
GBR	Great Britain	KOR	Korea
GRE	Greece	KUW	Kuwait
GRN	Grenada	KGZ	Kyrgyzstan
GUM	Guam	LAO	Lao People's Democratic Republic

NATIONAL OLYMPIC COMMITTEES RECOGNIZED BY
THE INTERNATIONAL OLYMPIC COMMITTEE

LAT	Latvia	NEP	Nepal
LIB	Lebanon	NED	Netherlands
LES	Lesotho	AHO	Netherlands Antilles
LBR	Liberia	NZL	New Zealand
LBA	Libya Arab Jamahiriya	NCA	Nicaragua
LIE	Liechtenstein	NIG	Niger
LTU	Lithuania	NGR	Nigeria
LUX	Luxembourg	NOR	Norway
MKD	Macedonia, Former Yugoslav Rep.	OMA	Oman
MAD	Madagascar	PAK	Pakistan
MAW	Malawi	PLE	Palestine
MAS	Malaysia	PAN	Panama
MDV	Maldives	PNG	Papua New Guinea
MLI	Mali	PAR	Paraguay
MLT	Malta	CHN	People's Republic of China
MTN	Mauritania	PRK	People's Republic of Korea
MRI	Mauritius	PER	Peru
MEX	Mexico	PHI	Philippines
MON	Monaco	POL	Poland
MGL	Mongolia	POR	Portugal
MAR	Morocco	PUR	Puerto Rico
MOZ	Mozambique	QAT	Qatar
MYA	Myanmar	MDA	Republic of Moldova
NAM	Namibia	NRU	Republic of Nauru

NATIONAL OLYMPIC COMMITTEES RECOGNIZED BY
THE INTERNATIONAL OLYMPIC COMMITTEE

TJK	Republic of Tajikistan	SUI	Switzerland
ROM	Romania	SYR	Syrian Arab Republic
RUS	Russian Federation	THA	Thailand
RWA	Rwanda	TOG	Togo
VIN	Saint Vincent and the Grenadines	TGA	Tonga
SMR	San Marino	TRI	Trinidad and Tobago
STP	Sao Tome and Principe	TUN	Tunisia
KSA	Saudi Arabia	TUR	Turkey
SEN	Senegal	TKM	Turkmenistan
SEY	Seychelles	UGA	Uganda
SLE	Sierra Leone	UKR	Ukraine
SIN	Singapore	UAE	United Arab Emirates
SVK	Slovakia	TAN	United Republic of Tanzania
SLO	Slovenia	USA	United States of America
SOL	Solomon Islands	URU	Uruguay
SOM	Somalia	UZB	Uzbekistan
RSA	South Africa	VAN	Vanuatu
ESP	Spain	VEN	Venezuela
SRI	Sri Lanka	VIE	Vietnam
SKN	St. Kitts and Nevis	ISV	Virgin Islands
LCA	St. Lucia, W.I.	SAM	Western Samoa
SUD	Sudan	YEM	Yemen
SUR	Surinam	YUG	Yugoslavia
SWZ	Swaziland	ZAI	Zaire
SWE	Sweden	ZAM	Zambia
Unknown to IOC		ZIM	Zimbabwe

ATLANTA
ON MY MIND
Stan Constantine

Arrangement: Steffan Morgan
and Nicolette Kost De Sevres

DREAMS___ THEY BE - COME TRUE ON YOUR DOOR-STEP IN THE WORLD OF GAL - AX -

MYSTERY OF STONE MOUNTAIN

Shakuhachi Flute Solo

Stan Constantine

Arr: Nicolette Kost De Sevres

318

SOCCER GAME IN ATHENS
Stan Constantine

Arrangement: Claude Mahen
and Nicolette Kost De Sevres

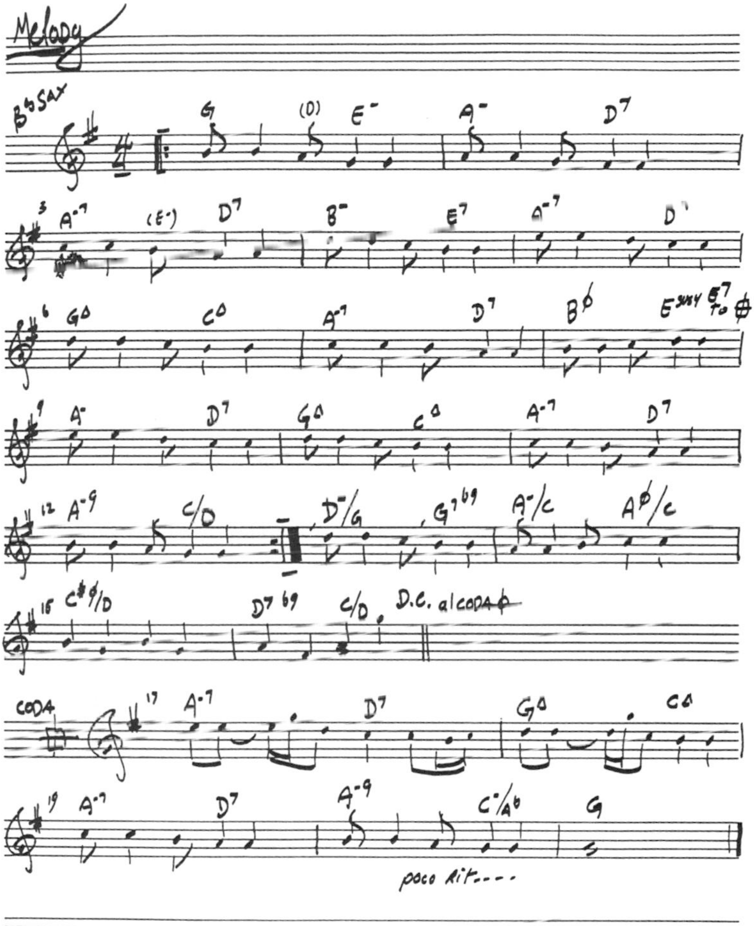

Mayfair MUSIC PUBLICATIONS INC.

AMERICAN WEDDING MARCH

Stan Constantine

Arr Nicolette Kost De Sevres

Glo-ria Glo-ria all to see___ for bet - ter___ or worse___ shall it be

Glo-ria Glo-ria our wed-ding Glo-ria Glo-ria our wed-ding Glo-ria Glo-ria all to see___ for bet - ter

or worse___ shall it be

D.C. al Fine

Fine

BRING ME FROM NIPPON

Stan Constantine

Arr. for Shakuhachi
Yoshio Masumoto

Arr. Steffan Morgan

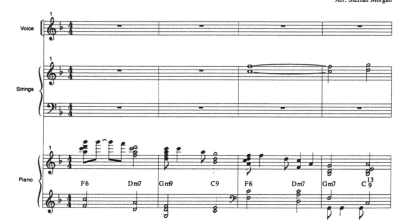

LOVE · LY ME-MEN-TO   BRING ME   C · CROSS THE   SUN · SPUN SEA

Bring Me From Nippon
Stan Constantine

(Japanese musical notation — tategaki)

数々の
KAZUKAZU NO

思い出の
OMOIDE NO

蘇る
YOMOGAERU

I get back a lot of my memories,

日の出る国
HI NO DERU KUNI

country of sunrise,

忘れられぬ
WASURE RARENU

夢の国
YUME NO KUNI

unforgettable dreamy country,

我が心の
WAGA KOKORO NO

故郷
FURUSATO

A place dear to my heart, NIPPON.

Arr. for Shakuhachi   Yoshio Masumoto
Masumoto - Shakuhachi Trio

乙　あ、あ〜　リ甲、ロ、ッ、ツ、
なチ甲、チレツ、ロ、つかしや
甲なヒ、ヒチ、レ、らおてら
ふヒ甲、じのチ、チ、たかね
ばんヒチ、ヒ、だのさくら
甲わたチ、チレツ、チチ、しのニッポン
おリ、もりロ甲、いでのレ
乙かリ、ずチ甲、かツ、のツ、
甲チ、みがツ、ずツ、える
より、ロ甲、ツ、ツ、
乙リ、リ、ロ甲、ツ、ツ、

I get back a lot of my memories,
蘇る
YOMIGAERU
数々の
KAZUKAZU NO
思い出の
OMOIDE NO
私のニッポン　My NIPPON,
WATASHI NO NIPPON
万朶の桜　countless cherry blossoms,
BANDA NO SAKURA
富士の高嶺　Mt. FUJI,
FUJI NO TAKANE
奈良のお寺　temples of NARA,
NARA NO OTERA
懐かしや　nostalgic rememberances, AH!
NATSUKASHIYA
嗚呼！

330

Bring Me From Nippon

Stan Constantine

I get back a lot of my memories,
蘇る
YOMOGAERU

数々の
KAZUKAZU NO

思い出の
OMOIDE NO

日の出る国
HI NO DERU KUNI
country of sunrise.

忘れられぬ
WASURE RARENU
unforgettable dreamy country,

夢の国
YUME NO KUNI

我が心の
WAGA KOKORO NO
A place dear to my heart, NIPPON.

故郷
FURUSATO

℗© Copyright Stan Constantine 1996

Arr. for Shakuhachi　Yoshio Masumoto
Masumoto - Shakuhachi Trio

リ、リ、ロ、ツ、ツ、
乙　リ、ロ、甲ツ、える
よ、み、が、
甲チ、甲チ、レ、ツ、
か、り、ず、ず、の
リ、ロ、甲か、ず、の
おり、もり、チ、レ、ツ、チ、
わ、た、し、の
甲チ、チ、レ、ツ、チチ、ニッポン
ヒチ、ヒ、ヒ、
ばんだの　さくら
甲ヒチ、ヒチ、チ、
ふ、じ、の　たかね
甲ヒ、ヒチ、レ、レ、
な、ら、の　おてら
チ、チレ、ツ、ロ、
なつかしや
乙甲リロ、ツ、
ああ〜

私のニッポン
WATASHI NO NIPPON

蘇る
YOMIGAERU

数々の
KAZUKAZU NO

思い出の
OMOIDE NO
My NIPPON,

万朶の桜
BANDA NO SAKURA
countless cherry blossoms,

富士の高嶺
FUJI NO TAKANE
Mt.FUJI,

奈良のお寺
NARA NO OTERA
temples of NARA,

懐かしや
NATSUKASHIYA
nostalgic rememberances, AH!

嗚呼！
AH!

I get back a lot of my memories,

332

SOUTHERN BIRDS
Stan Constantine

Arrangement: Claude Maheu
and Nicolette Kost De Sevres

DEPARTURE OF MARA

Music By
S. Constantine

Andante Sostenuto

ATLANTA ON MY MIND
American Potpourri

by Stan Constantine

1. ATLANTA ON MY MIND
   Soloists: Barbara Charest
   and Claude Maheu
2. MYSTERY OF STONE MOUNTAIN
   Soloist: Claude Maheu
3. WANDERING AMONG THE STARS
   Soloist: Wayne Robinson
4. SOCCER GAME IN ATHENS
   Soloists: Claude Maheu
   and Nicolette Kost De Sevres
5. BRING ME FROM NIPPON
   Soloists: Yoshio Masumoto
   and Masumoto Shirohachi Trio
6. SOUTHERN BIRDS
   Soloist: Nicolette Kost
   De Sevres

7. AMERICAN WEDDING MARCH
   Soloist: Barbara Charest
8. POTOMAC WALTZ
   Soloist: Wayne Robinson
9. LUCKY SEVEN
   Soloist: Jack Cohen
10. PRAIRIE POLKA
   Soloists: Wayne Robinson
   and Jack Cohen
11. EARLY WINTER
   Soloist: Wayne Robinson
12. I AM SO HAPPY
   Soloist: Jack Cohen
13. CHRISTMAS IN THE COUNTRY
   Soloist: Maria Delli Colli
14. JOURNEY HOME
   Soloist: Wayne Robinson

Sailing on Brain Waves